IT'S A GHOST'S LIFE

ERIN MCCARTHY

Copyright © 2019 by Erin McCarthy

Cover art by LLewellen Designs

All rights reserved.

No part of this book may be reproduced in any form or by any electronic or mechanical means, including information storage and retrieval systems, without written permission from the author, except for the use of brief quotations in a book review.

ONE

"BAILEY BURKE, do you solemnly swear to tell the truth, the whole truth, and nothing but the truth, so help you God?"

I cleared my throat. "I do."

"Does this dress make me look fat?" my best friend, Alyssa Dembowski, asked me, emerging from her dressing room at Saks.

Dicey question to pose to a man, but to ask me, her bestie since high school, it was no big deal. We knew how to be honest but delicate with each other. It is truly the girl code to not let your friend go out looking less than her best, but in this case, Alyssa was worrying for no reason. She looked fabulous in the red polka dots with her dark hair.

"No, you do not look fat. You look amazing and I'm completely jealous of your cleavage."

Alyssa eyed herself in the mirror and wrinkled her nose. "Vera makes me feel insecure."

I had to laugh, glancing over at Vera, who was draping herself in a fur coat that was approximately seven sizes too big for her. My grandma Burke was searching for the rack of cardigans that all looked exactly like the one million cardigans she already owned.

"Vera is ninety-five years old, Alyssa. Literally ninety-five. She had her birthday last October."

"Yeah, but look at her. She's stylish as hell and back in the day they called her 'Va Va Voom Vera.' She still somehow oozes sexual confidence. I feel frumpy next to her."

"That's insane. You are not frumpy."

"I'm old, but not deaf," Vera said, turning toward us and pushing up her enormous round black glasses. "I can hear both of you. Alyssa, a woman needs two things in life—confidence and a red lipstick. You've got the lips, now put your chin up and sell it."

That was something I personally sucked at. I go for cute, not an attempt to "sell it." I looked at myself in the mirror and saw a slight woman with wild red hair and fair skin, being swallowed by a puffy navy blue coat with a faux fur trim. It looked cheap next to Vera's palazzo pants, designer boots, fur, and expensive glasses and haircut. Just because it was January in Cleveland didn't mean I needed to give into schlumpy. I usually lived by that creed as well as Vera did but it had been a particularly harsh January and I was having post-Christmas blues.

All of which meant I just needed to do as Vera instructed Alyssa and put my chin up.

"Sell it. Got it," Alyssa said.

Vera came toward us and handed the fur to Alyssa. "Try this." To me, she said, "Found any dead bodies lately?"

"Not since before Christmas," I assured her.

Vera looked at Grandma Burke. "She looks so innocent."

"Margaret's always been competitive. It used to be medals at Irish dance competitions. Now it's dead people."

Um, what? "Grandma, I am not looking for dead people in a quest to be interesting." I wasn't even going to ask her not to use my middle name Margaret. She'd been doing it since I was born and my mother had the audacity to give me a non-Christian first name. Grandma Burke is Irish, she's stubborn, and if anyone is competitive, it's her. She wanted to out-do Vera, who generally speaking had had a much cooler life than my grandmother. Apparently, the plan was to do it vicariously through me and my unusual brushes with death of late.

Vera and Grandma Burke were an unlikely pair. Vera had grown up in Cleveland in a wealthy Jewish family before heading to Hollywood in her twenties and spending two decades modeling, acting in bit roles, and dating leading men. Eventually she'd come back and settled down, but still had her fair share of scandals and men well into her eighties. My grandmother had been married from twenty until my grandfather passed away, and prided herself on her soda bread and her ability to recite the rosary for hours on end.

They had met at the cardiologist's office at the Cleveland Clinic five years ago and for whatever reason, adored each other instantly. Now that I think about it, not much different from Alyssa and me. We have completely opposite personalities. Neither Grandma nor Vera drive anymore, and everyone on the road is thankful for that. But for a girls' day out of drinkie, shoppie, lunchie, as Alyssa called it, they needed me to drive. I didn't trust them to use Lyft or Uber. Vera would just walk up to a random car and demand they drive her somewhere without ever even downloading the app.

"So how do you explain you racking up dead bodies like pool balls?" Vera asked. She pulled the corner of the fur down off of Alyssa's shoulder. "Show some skin."

"I need somewhere to go to wear this," Alyssa said, turning and spinning, giving us all lots of shoulder. "I feel like a man killer right now."

"See? This is how you kill men," Vera told me. "Not the way you do it."

"I'm not killing anyone!" Geez, you have a couple of dead bodies under your nose and people start judging. I'd only found two bodies, and one was only a thigh and an arm, so did that even count? I'd seen a third dead body, shot while lounging by the lake in swim trunks, but that turned out to be a ghost, and not an actual body, so I'm sticking with two as my final number. "Besides, I have a boyfriend. I don't need to be a man killer."

"Oh, honey, that's where you're wrong. It's harder to *keep* a man than it is to get one. They all go for shiny and new. You have to stay shiny."

Great. Now Vera had me feeling as insecure as she had Alyssa.

I didn't worry a lot about losing Jake Marner, my super-hot detective boyfriend, but sometimes when he sighed, I suspected I tried him to the depths of his soul.

Because did I mention I see ghosts?

Marner sort of believes me but maybe not entirely, though he tries hard.

It started the day my best friend, and his partner, Ryan, showed up in my kitchen talking crap and mocking my weight loss. He'd been dead eight months and then suddenly there he was, like no big deal. Wearing work boots and a flannel shirt and telling me I needed to solve his murder.

Me, I'd thought it was a big deal. Because Ryan appearing to me was cool after my initial freak-out and had helped me get through some of my grief. But after Ryan appeared, so did other random ghosts and five months later it still stunned me to think that my life had become a hostess stand for the disenfranchised dead showing up for a table.

"Stay shiny. Will do." I gave Vera a thumbs-up.

She looked at me like I was a lunatic. "Let's go to lunch. I want a martini."

I did too because it had just occurred to me clear out of the blue the next day was the one-year anniversary of Ryan's death. I'd been so busy with Christmas and planning a trip to see my sister in Texas, and managing my home-staging business, "Put It Where?" that I hadn't realized the anniversary was so soon.

I gripped the zipper on my puffy coat and felt awash in emotion.

"The old lady's right," a voice said right behind me.

I jumped and whirled around. Ryan was standing there. "What?" I said out loud before I realized I couldn't have a conversation with a ghost in Saks without the disdainful sales woman calling for security.

"What what?" Vera asked me. "I said I want a martini. Get the lead out, doll. I could die before we reach the restaurant."

Grandma Burke touched my elbow. "Why don't you go ahead and get us a table. I'm going to stop at the restroom. I like the one here in Saks. Vera, why don't you come with me?" Grandma gave me a wink.

She saw Ryan too. She'd told me that when he reappeared at Christmas after getting an eviction notice from heaven. He still hadn't told me what he'd done to get tossed, but clearly, it wasn't good.

"I'm not wiping your ass," Vera told Grandma Burke. "If that's why you're asking."

"Of course not. I have a date next week and I want your advice, but not in front of my granddaughter."

That made me forget entirely about Ryan. "What? You have a *date*?" I said, scandalized. "With who?"

My grandmother didn't date. She martyred herself at the feet of widowhood. Besides, it was unlikely she'd find a man as willing to let her boss him around as my grandfather had.

"See what I mean?" Grandma asked Vera. "She's nutso."

"I understand. One of the many reasons I never had children," Vera said. "So self-centered."

Now I was self-centered as well as being an attention-seeker going off in search of dead bodies? That seemed a little harsh.

"I'll be at the checkout desk," Alyssa said after Grandma and Vera shuffled off in pursuit of the restroom.

Suddenly Grandma's gesture to leave me alone with Ryan seemed thoroughly unimportant compared to the fact that she had a date. "She better be joking," I said out loud.

"Why? Can't an old lady get laid?" Ryan asked.

He always managed to incite my outrage, even as a ghost. "I beg your pardon," I said, sounding nothing like a twenty-eight-year-old, and every inch ancient British aristocracy. "How dare you."

Ryan laughed. "You are so easy to get riled up. I love that about you."

"Glad I can amuse you. Why are you at Saks?" I asked, pretending like I was talking into my cell phone. People tend to look strangely at you if you have long one-sided conversations with yourself in public, because unlike lucky me, most people didn't see Ryan or any of the other ghosts who had been traipsing in and out of my life. "Do you need cuff links to wear for your ceremonial fall from grace?"

He raised his eyebrows. "Wow, you are tense today. Marner not slipping it to you lately?"

That was not the way to improve my mood. Ryan teased me mercilessly about dating Jake, and for his part, Jake frequently appeared jealous of my friendship with his former partner. Even though Ryan was dead. Not that I could blame him. Before Ryan died, I had been harboring a pretty mega-sized crush on him. I might have possibly even confessed to loving him before trying to kiss him. One year ago tomorrow. Egad.

Ever since Ryan had reappeared to me right before Christmas, Marner had been more pensive than usual. He seemed remote and that was a big bag of yuck. I didn't like feeling like he was retreating away from me. Especially after I had endured the presence of a leg lamp for the majority of the holiday decorating season purely out of love for him.

"It's a year tomorrow," I said testily.

"I am well aware of that fact. Which is why you should be nice to me and not bitchy."

Ryan had a special talent for making me feel guilty. "I'm not trying to be bitchy. I'm sad."

"Don't be sad, Bai. Shit happens. But I'll be over tomorrow because we have to talk about our assignment. I'm catching a lot of crap upstairs and I need to take this seriously."

"Take what seriously?"

But he just gave me a wink. "Gotta go, yo. I'd like fried chicken, mashed potatoes, and cheesecake for my death anniversary dinner."

"You can't even eat solids."

"I want to smell it."

"That's very morbid."

"Tomahto, tomayto. Get some vitamin D, by the way. You look pale."

Probably because I was picturing my boyfriend's reaction to me cooking dinner. I'm not a very good cook. I eat a lot of string cheese and chicken nuggets. My meals solo tend to look like a grade school lunch.

Ryan didn't bother to wait for my answer though because he was already gone. Alyssa came over to me with a giant bag in her hand.

"Why did I just buy a dress I don't need and three pairs of shoes?"

"Vera pressure."

"Indeed." Alyssa, who was something of a serial dater, had been on a hiatus since she'd revenge-dated a bully from high school and then had accidently caught feelings for him. "I need to go back on a dating app. I cannot fathom the idea of spending Valentine's Day alone this year. I have four weeks to get a guy to the point where he's groomed to handle the big V Day without flipping out about it."

I glanced at my phone. How long had Vera and Grandma been gone? Was this a fallen-and-can't-get-up situation? "Do you seriously care about Valentine's Day? I thought you always said it was commercial hype."

"It is. But I need to post pictures of myself with a hottie so that Michael can see I'm happy."

Hello. Dating to make someone else jealous did not seem like a recipe for a romantic Valentine's Day. "There is so much wrong with what you just said. What I'm going to say is this—I'm supposed to be the insecure one, not you."

Alyssa made a face. "I'm not insecure. I'm just determined. Besides, don't come at me with relationship advice just because you have a case of the 'we's."

"What the heck is that?"

"We went to dinner. We are going to the beach. We ate breakfast in bed. We spend our Saturday nights in pjs giggling on the couch together. You and Jake. You're 'we' people now."

I was not going to take this personally. I had a feeling Alyssa was actually, quite possibly, in love with Michael and she needed to work that out. Also, she wasn't totally wrong about me and Jake. We were a little gushy with each other. Well, before Ryan had reappeared and Jake had decided that his getting up at five in the morning was interrupting my sleep too much and he'd started spending more nights at his apartment.

The thought made me wrinkle my nose. "Tomorrow is one year since Ryan died," I said.

"Oh, shit, that's right." Alyssa bit her lip. "Are you okay?"

I shrugged. "I guess. I mean, I miss him." I did miss him being alive. But his ghost helped take the sting away a little. "It's hard. I don't even want to think about how his parents and his sister are going to be feeling."

"You know I suck at that kind of stuff. You're at least tactful. I'm better at getting people drunk than comforting them."

Very true. "We all have our strengths. It doesn't help right now that I feel like my parents hate each other and I'm worried about me and Jake."

"Why are you worried about Jake? And your parents have hated each other for years, I wouldn't stress about that."

That almost made me laugh. "So I'm not the only one who has noticed?"

Alyssa raised her eyebrows. "Bailey. Your father cannot say anything without your mom saying the polar opposite."

"Very true." If my father said it was cold outside when it was ten below she'd say it was because his circulation was poor from spending the seventies and eighties smoking. There was nothing he could do that was worthy of anything other than a correction, in my mother's point of view. "I'm worried about Jake because he used to spend almost every night at my place and now he's spending more than half the week at his apartment. He says it's because he doesn't want to interrupt my sleep but I feel like there's more to it."

Alyssa didn't know that I saw ghosts and I was frankly terrified to tell her. I wasn't even sure why. She was pretty open to live and let live. She'd probably find it fascinating. But I hesitated because she was a data analyst who loved math and science and in the past had expressed skepticism over the paranormal.

"Don't be paranoid. He's being nice to you, that's all. Or maybe your mattress sucks or something. If it bothers you, tell him you'd rather have him there than quality sleep."

That was Alyssa. She just came straight out and said what she was thinking. I was afraid to bring it up with Jake because I was afraid what his response might be. I shrugged, noncommittal. "Okay, I'm going to find Grandma and Vera. This is taking forever."

They were both applying lipstick in front of the mirror and Vera was describing in shocking detail what she had done to her third husband backstage at the Oscars in '63. She spotted me and said to my reflection, without turning around, "Stay shiny, remember?"

"DO YOU THINK I'M SHINY?" I asked Jake later that night as we sat at a local sports bar in Lakewood near his apartment.

"Hmm?" He was staring at the eight TV screens watching basketball. He wrested his gaze away from the game and glanced at me up and down. "I guess your nose is a little oily, but it's not bad."

See? This was precisely why I was afraid to ask him anything. "That's not what I meant," I said, even as I raised my hand to swipe at my nose, fearful I was looking like I'd been dipped in Crisco. After a whole afternoon of listening to Vera's romantic escapades and worrying myself to total paranoia that Jake no longer found me attractive, I had taken extra time with my hair and makeup.

I was also wearing a sweater and skinny jeans in dark colors that were a tight and sexy departure from my usual florals. Jake had given me a whistle when he'd picked me up but after that seemed to have forgotten that I existed.

"What did you mean?" he asked, glancing back at the TV before blinking at me, obviously confused.

"They say men like something shiny and new all the time. Am I shiny?"

Jake opened his mouth and shut it again. "I have no idea what you're talking about." His eyes drifted back to the basketball game.

I sighed and picked up my gin fizz and sucked at the tiny straw. "You know what tomorrow is, don't you?"

"Sunday."

I sucked harder. "It's the day Ryan died."

That got his attention. He swirled his stool to be facing me. "Are you okay?"

"I don't know." I didn't. I had thought I was okay but I felt... weird. "Are you okay?"

He nodded. "I'm still pissed and upset and I miss Ryan, but it is what it is."

I wrinkled my nose. "Are *we* okay?"

"Why wouldn't we be okay?"

I shrugged.

Jake took my hand and caressed the back of it. "Babe, what exactly are we talking about? I know you had feelings for Ryan. But I thought we had moved past that."

Now I was the one who didn't know what we were talking about. "Sure. Do you want fried chicken for dinner tomorrow?"

He shook his head back and forth like a dog after a bath. "What? What the hell happened today? You go to lunch with the ladies and you come home broken."

He was trying to make light of all of this.

Yet I couldn't help but be insulted.

I gasped. "That's not cute or funny." My phone hang on the bar top and I saw it was my grandmother. She was normally the only person I would answer when I was with my boyfriend. But given how our current conversation was going I probably would have answered a telemarketer.

"Hello?" It was almost eleven o'clock. My grandmother shouldn't even be awake. "Grandma, are you okay?"

I could hear her sniffling, which instantly terrified me. I sat up straighter.

"Oh, Bailey, it's Vera."

"What about Vera?" I covered my left ear with my palm so I could hear her better. It was loud in the bar.

"She's dead."

My stomach dropped. I whirled around, half expecting to see Vera standing behind me in ghost form. "What?" I said, shocked to the tips of my pointed-toe boots. "We just spent the day with her!"

"They found her in the backyard, frozen like a popsicle."

My jaw went south just like my stomach had. "Oh my God."

I smacked Jake's leg. "Vera's dead."

"Well, shit."

My feelings exactly.

TWO

"WHAT HAPPENED?" I asked Grandma. "Who found her?"

"Her neighbor's dog was barking nonstop so he went out his back door to holler at him and it set his motion light off. He glanced over at Vera's and there she was—head first in the snow."

I shuddered. "Oh my God, that's horrible. Why would she go outside like that?"

"I have no clue. Her dog died last fall so she shouldn't have any reason to go out in weather like this."

That *was* disturbing. It was January and freezing. The kind of weather where it feels like your lungs are crystallizing when you breathe outside. "What have the cops said?"

"I don't know. Bob, her neighbor, just called me and let me know and asked me if I knew who her next of kin was."

"Who is it?"

"She has a niece who lives in Florida and a nephew in New York City. I don't know about anyone else other than her stepson, but he's in L.A. and not a blood relative."

I sipped my drink, feeling horrible. Obviously, it wasn't a total shock that someone at ninety-five could die, but Vera had been *fine* that afternoon. It made no sense. "Can I do anything to help?"

"Can you take me to church tomorrow? I want to say a prayer

for her and I'd rather you take me than your mother. She didn't like Vera."

Some days I wasn't sure who my mother liked. "Of course. Ten o'clock mass?"

"Eight."

I mentally groaned. I can't say I've ever been close friends with the morning. "Got it. See you then, and, Grandma, I'm really sorry about Vera. She was a very cool person."

"Thank you, dear."

I could tell she was struggling not to cry. When I ended the call I turned to Jake. "That's completely bizarre. My grandmother said Vera was in her back yard. Who goes into their backyard at night in the dead of January?"

"Did she smoke?" Jake asked.

"I don't think so, but honestly, Vera is old school enough that if she wanted to smoke she'd do it in her house or her garage. She had one of those townhome-style condos. Her garage is attached and her backyard is a paver patio with a small patch of grass behind it. Thank God the neighbor's dog was barking. He found her when he opened the door to yell at his dog and the motion light turned on."

"I'm sorry, babe." Jake squeezed my knee. "That sucks. At least you got to spend time with her today."

I nodded, distracted. All I could think was that this didn't make sense. "Don't you think it's weird?" I insisted.

Marner is a homicide detective. I was surprised he wasn't more suspicious. He paused for a heartbeat, then said, "Where did Vera live? Cleveland proper?"

I shook my head. "Bratenahl." It was a small enclave surrounded by Cleveland and Lake Erie, known for lakefront mansions and high-end condos.

"Do you want me to call their department and get more details?"

"Could you?" I asked, relieved. "This just feels... off." I wasn't sure what I was implying, exactly, just that Vera wasn't outdoorsy in the summer. Why the hell would she be going for a stroll outside in the dead of winter. Ugh. Dead of winter. Poor choice of words.

"I'm going to step outside and call them. It's too loud in here. You wait here, babe. It's too cold for you."

Jake was considerate about things like that. He knew I was a huge winter wimp. "Thank you. I love you."

His eyes got dark. "I love you too. Be right back."

Restless, while waiting, I went into my camera roll and pulled up the picture of Grandma and Vera that I had impulsively snapped that afternoon. My vision blurred and I pulled my vape out of my purse and sucked on it. Technically, you weren't supposed to in the bar, but I'd seen like five other people do it already. I usually left it at home to resist temptation but now I was glad I had it.

It was just too much. Vera had seemed so vibrant. So alive. Now she was gone. And tomorrow marked the one-year anniversary of Ryan's death. I felt grief wash over me like an ice-cold wave.

Jake came back while I was clutching my phone to my chest and sobbing.

"Maybe we should go," he said, gently. He lifted his hand for the bartender. "Sorry," he told him. "I need to cash out. We got some bad news."

The bartender took one look at me blubbering and waved his hand. "It's on me, no worries. Sorry for your news."

"Thanks, man." Jake dropped some money on the bar top for a tip and helped me off my stool.

Blind from my tears and making an embarrassing hiccupping sound I couldn't seem to control, I stumbled in my high-heeled boots. Jake caught me.

"Sweetheart, that is not what we talked about. Pull it together."

Whirling around at the sound of Vera's voice, I saw her standing three feet away in a very plain nightgown and cheetah print boots. Designer boots. Expensive as hell. Two grand kind of expensive. "Vera."

Her hair and makeup were fully done up. She blew me a kiss

and gave me a wink. Then she was gone. There was a time I thought I might get used to ghosts just dropping in wherever I was, but nope. It was like when you were chilling on your couch and a spider runs across your arm. You freak the freak out.

But I also realized instantly that what Vera had just been wearing in front of me was what she'd been wearing when she died. Every ghost who had appeared to me so far had been trapped in their final outfit (good reason to keep it classy, people).

But now I knew something was shady. Vera would never step into a snowdrift in a pair of mohair high-heel boots. "What did the cops say?" I asked Jake as he gently but firmly pulled me toward the door.

"They said it appears she was dazed and confused, stepped outside, and the door automatically locked behind her and she couldn't get back in."

I clapped my hand over my mouth. "What? That's horrible! Why wouldn't she just go knock on the neighbor's back door?"

"They feel it was an episode of dementia." Marner pushed open the door and waited for me to walk past him.

I regretted not putting on my coat sooner. I shivered and shoved my arms through the sleeves. His response was troubling to me. Vera did not have dementia. She had her shit together more than half the people I knew. "That doesn't make sense. She was totally lucid this afternoon. Just hours ago."

"Babe, she was old. The mind comes and goes at that age."

I zipped my coat up and yanked my hood over my head. "How long does it take to die in weather like this?" The thought of Vera out there, confused, freezing to death, made my stomach turn.

"At her age? Probably not long considering they found her in a thin nightgown."

Here was my opening. "Was she wearing shoes?"

He nodded as he unlocked his car and opened the passenger door for me. "Boots."

That was not specific enough. That could be anything from galoshes to snow boots to go-go boots. "What kind of boots?"

Jake frowned at me. "I don't know. Bailey, what are you worrying about exactly?"

"It just doesn't make sense," I insisted. "Are they going to do an autopsy?"

He didn't answer me. Just shut the door and came around to the driver's side. He turned the car on and cranked up the heat. Rubbing his palms together he turned to me. "They're not treating it as a suspicious death. She was an old lady with a ton of medications in her kitchen and bathroom. Maybe she heard a noise outside, forgot it was January, forgot her door auto-locks, and didn't know what to do. I don't think there will be much of an investigation."

"Can we ask for an autopsy?"

He shook his head. "No. Her family has to do that if the department doesn't intend to." He shifted into "reverse" and asked, "My place, right?"

"Yes." I didn't want to be alone and we were only a few blocks from his apartment. I kept glancing in the back seat of his car, hopeful that Vera might appear. Marner might not like or totally believe that I spoke to the dead, but I could care less about his opinion on it at the moment. I needed answers from Vera.

"Vera wouldn't go outside in those boots," I told him. "Those are Saint Laurent and they're over two thousand dollars for a pair. She wouldn't ruin those."

Jake sighed. "First of all, how do you know what boots she was wearing? I didn't tell you that because the detective didn't tell *me*. Not that I would know what the hell whatever French crap you just said is anyway. He just said boots."

"I saw Vera at the bar. She appeared behind us for just a second."

"Jesus," was Jake's response. "What are you saying you think happened to her? Someone threw her out the back door and locked her out?"

"I don't know what I'm saying." I didn't. Who would want to

kill Vera? "Were there any signs of burglary? She probably has cash sitting around."

"They didn't say that, no."

"So we don't know for sure."

Jake paused. "No."

"Can you ask?"

"Can't you just ask Vera?" He waved his hand around. "Hi, Vera, nice to meet you."

"She's not here now," I said, frowning. "Are you even listening to me?"

Marner snorted. "Oh, yeah, I'm listening to you. I'm hearing everything you're saying."

He thought I was overreacting, clearly. I blew out a breath and tried to calm myself down. I didn't want to fight with my boyfriend. Not when I had better things to do.

Like solve Vera's homicide.

It had to be murder.

I didn't buy the dementia bit. At all.

I would just have to pick my way around this delicately, with Grandma's help.

We pulled into the driveway of the duplex Marner lived in. His apartment was upstairs and we didn't spend as much time here as we did at my house because his downstairs neighbors had just had a baby and they were cranky about my high heels and other, ahem, sounds that might drift down to them. My house in Ohio City is a free-standing Victorian. The neighbors are close, but we don't share walls.

As soon as he opened the front door downstairs, I knew the drill. Remove the high-heeled boots. I almost fell over trying to pull them off in the narrow alcove. Jake had hooks there for coats and I reluctantly divested myself of my puffy coat and hung it. Then I ran quickly up the wood stairs in my socks, intending to dive onto the couch and under a blanket.

"Where are you going?" Jake asked. "I kind of thought we'd go right to bed."

I knew what that meant. "Forget it, Detective," I told him. "I'm not getting naked. It's three degrees outside."

His eyebrows shot up. "So no fun until the cold spell snaps? Are you kidding me? I can work around flannel, I swear."

As charming as that sounded, I wasn't exactly in the mood. "In the morning, I promise. I'll be all warm and cozy then. Honestly, I'm too sad right now."

That made him contrite. He came over and sat next to me and pulled me against his chest. "I'm sorry, babe. I didn't realize how much Vera meant to you."

I snuggled against him. "It's just that you know, you have this fascinating life, and then you die alone in the cold? It's horrible. Did you know she was friends with Audrey Hepburn?"

"Wow, that's pretty amazing."

Jake was always pretty skilled at just letting me talk and showing the appropriate level of interest. Well, except when sports were on. But he let me ramble now. "She was married four times, but she used to joke it should only count as three because she married the same bastard twice. He was her second and fourth husband."

"How does that work? Geez."

"Apparently not well since it ended in divorce twice. But that never seemed to bother her. She painted her life as a great adventure instead of any sort of failure." I loved that confidence she had. Vera really had been the person who rolled through her life without guilt or regrets. I wish. I could feel guilty for weeks for accidentally letting a door close in someone's face.

"That's how it should be. So she went to Hollywood to be an actress?"

"Yes. But honestly, I think she went more for the parties. I don't think it ever bothered her that she never hit it big. She enjoyed everything she did."

Jake squeezed me closer. "You know who else did that?"

I glanced up at him. Jake has a strong jaw and dark eyes. They were filled with tenderness right now. "Who?"

"Ryan."

My heart squeezed. "Yeah. He did."

I half expected Ryan to show up and mock our sentimentality. When he didn't, I kissed Jake.

I was warmer already.

GRANDMA WORE BLACK TO CHURCH, of course. I sat through the mass with her, going through the familiar movements learned from a childhood of kneeling, standing, shaking hands. Growing up Catholic is like being in a club. Lots of rules and rituals. Plus bingo and doughnuts. The Ladies Guild sold doughnuts and coffee after mass down in the gaping basement reception hall slash bingo parlor. I remembered when they had banned smoking at bingo. You would have thought the plagues had descended on Cleveland. The eleventh being the Plague of No Smoking.

"I want a crawler," Grandma said. "They know to put one aside for me. If some snot-nosed kid snagged the last one I'm going to be PO'd."

Keeping it Christian, as usual.

"I can't walk any faster," I told her. "There's no crowd control." It was all ancients shuffling, kids zipping through legs, and soccer moms greeting all their fellow PTA moms.

Whenever anyone asked me if I was ready to have children, moments like the three-year-old wiping his tears on the back of his mother's ass assured me I was most decidedly not ready. I was still in that selfish phase where I preferred my clothes minus bodily fluids from offspring, okay, thanks.

Speaking of offspring, without warning I spotted Jake's mother. Shoot. What the hell— heck, I mean, we were still on church grounds—was she doing there? She belonged to a different parish fifteen minutes east. There was no way out of it. She had seen me and was waving.

Don't get me wrong. I like Jake's mother. I could even go so far as to say I liked Jake's mother more than my own. She wasn't judgmental like mine. She was kind, loving, baked lots of goodies, and laughed with abandon. She excelled at being a mother, and was a dream grandmother to Jake's nieces and nephews, always willing to babysit but without being an interfering busybody.

Thus, the problem.

Jake was turning thirty in two months, and until me, I think she'd thought he was approaching his expiration date as a fresh husband. That he was souring and was going to be tossed in the "not keepable" marital trash. Ever since we'd started dating, she'd been telling me she didn't understand why he hadn't found a nice girl before me, that he was good-looking, right? To which of course I nod "yes" every time. She then lists his many virtues, but ultimately concludes at the end of this speech on each occasion that it was his job as a homicide detective that was scaring off women. "Except for you," she then says. Every. Time. While patting my arm affectionately.

She wants us married and procreating, STAT.

He's her only son and she's worried he'll morph into creepy aging bachelor.

Or something like that.

Normally I really don't mind. I dodge the questions and implications but now I was feeling emotionally vulnerable because of Ryan's death anniversary (if that's a thing) and Vera's, in my mind, sketchy death.

"Hello, Bailey, sweetie," she said as we finally hit the bottom of the basement steps and could spread out a little. She reached out and gave me a hug. "What brings you here?"

"Hi," I said, hugging her back. "I brought my grandmother to mass this morning." I pointed in the direction of Grandma Burke, who had made a beeline for the crawlers. She could move fast with the right motivation. "A friend of hers passed away last night and she wanted company today."

"Oh, no, how sad. But how sweet of you." Her look was one of genuine concern. Jake's mom has good genes, which I admit has crossed my mind more than once. Good genetics to pass on, right?

But at sixty-two she looked a decade younger. She rode her bike, did Pilates, and baked giant Italian pasta meals with an enviable balance.

"What are you doing here?" I asked.

"I'm going to brunch with my best friend from high school, Susan. We went to St. Augustine's together so I just decided to go to mass with her." She gave me a wink. "Then mimosas."

"That sounds fun."

"Mrs. M, what's up?"

The male voice made me jump. Dang it. That was Ryan. It took everything I had not to turn around and acknowledge him. Let's just all admit that espionage is not in my future.

"Gotta dash, sweetie. Let's make plans for dinner. I haven't seen Jake since the New Year. Bad son." She laughed. "Oh, and call me so we can make plans for Jake's thirtieth."

That also startled me. Were we doing that? Planning parties for him together? Apparently, we were. I didn't even know what kind of party Jake would want, if any, to be totally honest. Bad girlfriend.

We hugged again and said goodbye and then she went to find her friend. I ignored Ryan and went to find coffee. It tasted stale and slightly like cardboard, but I needed it. Coffee junkie, I totally admit it. I sucked down half of it before turning around to face the room at large. I was in the corner by the garbage can. The only people near me where random children who came running up with empty cups and tossed them in the can.

I got splashed with orange juice when a toddler misjudged distance but I didn't even care. I felt morose. Grandma had gone off to chat with her friends, double-fisting doughnuts.

"Are you ignoring me?" Ryan asked. "Rude."

He leaned against the back wall next to me and crossed his ankles.

"No, I'm not ignoring you. It's just hard to talk with a hundred people around." I glanced at him. "Are you supposed to be here? I thought you were in trouble and this is holy ground."

"This is a bingo parlor and doughnut hall. This is not holy ground. But I don't know if I could go upstairs in the sanctuary or not. I haven't tried. I spent enough time in church as a kid and we all know there's no saving my soul now."

"There isn't?" That was disturbing. I eyed him. "I thought that was the whole point. Of you being back here, I mean."

"I don't actually know what the point of me being back here is. Haven't figured that out yet. I just know I got showed the door in heaven and found myself back in your kitchen."

Lucky for both of us.

"So you and Mrs. M planning a big surprise party for Marner, huh? You know he hates that kind of shit."

Ryan had a way of making me feel completely insecure without even intending to. Or maybe he did intend to. Huh. Interesting thought.

"No one said surprise party. And yes, I am aware that is not his type of thing." He was far too even-tempered to get any sort of enjoyment out of an over-the-top reveal. "I know you hate it, but I do know Jake pretty well."

"Gross," was Ryan's opinion.

I rolled my eyes at him. "Listen, do you have any intel on Grandma's friend, Vera? She died last night and I think she was murdered." Ryan tended to hear through the grapevine whether someone was classified as murdered or natural death.

"I'm kind of on the outs right now. I'm not getting a lot of information from the higher-ups."

That was disappointing. "Shoot. I'm not sure what to do."

"Why do you think it was homicide?"

I explained my reasoning.

Ryan nodded. "I could see that. But it's more likely she just locked herself out. We can take a look at it though if you want."

That felt like a dismissal. A bit of a pat on the head even if he didn't mean that.

"Thanks." My throat closed. I felt like I should say something about the date. "Hey, um, don't think I've forgotten what day it is.

I'm just not sure what to say. Hallmark doesn't make a card for this, you know?"

Ryan pushed off the wall and gave me a closed-lip smile. "Don't worry about it, Bai. It is what it is."

That was what Jake had said.

"Maybe I don't want it to be what it is," I said, softly.

A little girl with brown curls appeared, ready to toss her doughnut wax paper into the trash. "Who are you talking about?" she asked.

Startled, I panicked, which is very me. "Jesus," I said.

Ryan burst out laughing.

"I was praying," I clarified to the girl. That wasn't far off the truth.

She nodded. "Do you need a hug?"

She couldn't be more than five years old. She was wearing striped leggings and a navy blue dress over them. There was a red bow in her hair.

I reached down and opened my arms. "I would love a hug."

She smelled like shampoo and sugar and her hug was sweet and steady.

My ovaries might have fluttered, just a little.

There might be something to this mom thing. Later, much later.

When I stood back up and waved as she skipped back to her family, Ryan was gone.

SINCE I MISSED ALL the doughnuts (those kids and seniors move fast), I talked Grandma into going to brunch with me close to my parents' house. After we were settled at a table and I had ordered a mimosa, I eyed my grandmother.

"Do you think Vera got confused? Does that seem possible to you?"

"Heck no. Vera hadn't lost her marbles. At all. Sure, I could see getting locked outside by accident but why would she go out there in the first place? Plus she has a cell phone and neighbors close by on either side."

My thoughts exactly. "I wonder if her phone was found on her. I think we need to call her niece and suggest an autopsy."

But Grandma shook her head. "I'm not calling her. You call her."

"Why? They don't even know me."

"They don't know me either! I'm sorry for your loss, and by the way, you should have your aunt cut open like a fish at the market? No, missy. I'm not doing it." She shook her head rapidly.

I have to admit, I was a little surprised. Grandma was not usually one to shy away from an awkward situation. But she did have a healthy dose of superstition about death, so maybe that was it.

"Fine. Give me her niece's number."

Okay, so Grandma wasn't wrong. It was very awkward. But once we got past the initial condolences and the niece's confusion as to who I was and why I cared, tension eased. Vera's niece's name was Eva, and she sounded like she was in her fifties or sixties.

"I tried to get Vera to move down here to Ft. Lauderdale," Eva said, "but she refused. I didn't understand it because it's freezing in Cleveland half the year and we don't have any family there anymore at all, but you know Vera. No one was going to tell her what to do."

For all her reticence, Grandma was now listening with an eagle ear. "What's she saying?"

I waved her off. "It's my understanding Vera wanted to stay independent."

"That is very true. Listen, this is uncomfortable," Eva said. "But Vera had a lot of really valuable items in her possession and I'm not suggesting anything, honestly I'm not, but she has that housekeeper who has a key, and who knows where everything is... since I can't get there until Tuesday, is there any way you and your grandmother could ask her for the key back? Or change the locks?"

Not suggesting anything, huh?

I rolled my eyes. I wasn't sure why she trusted us over a housekeeper Vera trusted, but in this case, it worked to my advantage. I would have access to search the townhouse. "We'd be happy to help any way we can."

"Great. I'll send you the housekeeper's number. I really need to do an inventory of everything and I want to make sure nothing is... disturbed in the meantime."

I got it. Vera had expensive jewelry, clothes, furs. Probably antiques and china. But Eva seemed more than a little concerned about securing it. Interesting. Mercenary niece has Vera bumped off? Plausible, but risky because she'd have to hire a thug to carry out the dirty deed.

"The police don't seem to find the circumstances of her death suspicious. Do you?" I asked.

"What?" she asked sharply. "Do you think she was being robbed?"

"It crossed my mind. I haven't seen the townhome, and the police don't seem to think it was tossed like a burglary scene would be, but I find it very odd for Vera to step into two feet of snow in her Saint Laurent cheetah print boots."

Eva gasped. "She was wearing the Saint Laurent boots? No." She followed that with a groan.

I wasn't sure if she was upset because she agreed with me it was odd, or if she was lamenting they had gone to the morgue with Vera, ruined. "With just a thin summer nightgown. It doesn't add up to me. Do you think maybe you should ask for an autopsy?"

"I hadn't thought..." Eva sounded confused and concerned, easing my suspicions of her. "I mean, do you think it's necessary? She was ninety-five years old. What would be the point?"

"If something happened to her and it was a robbery situation you would want recourse," I said vaguely. I just wanted to get her thinking.

"Oh good Lord. This is a mess. Let me call my brother. I'll text you the housekeeper's information."

After we said goodbye and I ended the call, Grandma Burke shook her head. "Margaret, I think you're stirring up trouble."

I hated the idea that even my grandmother thought I was a nutjob.

"But I love it," Grandma added. "Someone's got to do something. If Vera was pushed outside, someone needs to be strung up by their toenails." She reached over the table and grabbed my mimosa and took a hefty swallow. "Only yellow-livered bastards hurt kids and old ladies."

"I agree. That's why I can't let this go until we know it was truly an accident. Did you know Vera had a housekeeper?"

"Sure. Her name is Pam."

"Then I think it's time we had a little chat with Pam."

Good God, I was starting to sound like Colombo.

THREE

"WHEN ARE YOU BRINGING GRANDMA HOME?" my mother demanded.

"Uh..." I glanced over at Grandma in the passenger seat of my car as we pulled into Vera's townhome to wait for Pam. We were a good thirty minutes from my parents' house at this point and we still needed to poke around inside Vera's. "A bit later."

"Bailey, what on earth? You know you can't keep her out all day. She'll be cranky as hell when you bring her back here."

My mother's voice was so loud Grandma heard her and gave a snort. "She's the cranky one, not me."

"Mom, we're having fun." Or something like that.

"That's morbid," she said, and hung up on me.

"We're morbid," I told Grandma.

"Better than what I'd call her."

That made me laugh. "Right?"

I saw a car pull up. "Oh, I think this is Pam, the housekeeper."

Grandma and I got out of the car and met Pam in the driveway.

Pam didn't look like a thief who would kill an old lady to steal her jewelry. She looked like a preschool teacher. All wide-eyed concern and hand over her heart. "I can't believe it. When Eva called me, I was just in shock. Vera was so full of life. It didn't seem like her time."

It was possible Pam was a crackerjack actress. It was also more likely she was genuinely caught off guard.

"I know," I said, tone sympathetic. "I'm so sorry."

"Wasn't her time?" Grandma said, pulling her coat tighter around her. "She was ninety-five. When would be her time?"

Pam gave a startled laugh. "Well, that's true. It's just Vera seemed so strong and fiery." She held up the house key. "Eva said to give the key to you. I guess that's okay. She didn't have any other family and if that's what Eva wants... I told her I could still keep my cleaning schedule so things don't get too dusty but she wasn't interested."

I felt bad for Pam losing her job. She probably came to Vera's once a week. "Would you mind coming in with us and seeing if anything seems... disturbed? Not to be suspicious but none of us would know if an EMT lifted a Rolex." I felt guilty slurring the first responders but I needed something of an inventory and Pam was my best shot.

She also might get nervous if I was poking around Vera's drawers and give herself away if she had been the one to give Vera a heave-ho then snagged a bunch of expensive jewelry on her way out.

"Oh, sure. I can do that." Pam glanced toward her car. "I do have plans this afternoon."

"We won't be long," I assured her. I had to cook fried chicken for Ryan to smell. Or, realistically, stop at a chicken joint on the way home.

"Okay, then. I guess I can take a peek."

Vera's townhome was hushed and still. I hated that feeling inside a house... it's like the air hangs, waiting for something. Or someone. Like the house already knows no one is returning to it. I shivered. My mother was right. I was morbid.

The décor was exactly as I would have expected it—eclectic and expensive. There were antiques mixed with mid-century modern furnishings and black-and-white photography. It was done the way Vera had lived. Without rules.

"Everything in here looks fine," Pam said. "Nothing is disturbed or anything. The back patio is off the kitchen."

Grandma had picked up a vase and glanced at the bottom of it. She set it back down and followed us into the kitchen. The cabinets were Brazilian cherry and the countertops a very flashy granite with lots of sparkles in it. Nothing was noteworthy about the kitchen except for the bistro table in the corner. It was littered with pill bottles. Some were spilled onto the glass top.

"Does she always keep her pills on the kitchen table?" I asked, gesturing.

Pam shook her head. "No. She has a little dispenser in her bedroom. On Sundays she counts them out for the week and puts them in a compartment for each day so she doesn't get confused. But I'm not here regularly, now that I say that. I only know what she's told me. I really don't know how she lives day to day."

"Vera was no pill popper," Grandma said, defending her friend. "This looks fishy to me. What are all of these?"

Since the police had no intention of investigating, I figured it didn't matter if I took a look at the bottles. I read the labels without touching them though, just in case there were prints from the killer on them. "Vicodin. Ambien. Acebutolol. So pain killers, sleeping pills, and... I don't know that last one."

"High blood pressure," Grandma said.

Would that stuff be deadly taken together? I had no clue. I guess too much of anything can kill you. "Hmm," I said, noncommittal. I didn't want to speculate too much in front of Pam anyway.

I went over to the patio door. It was a French door that swung out. It was weird to me that she would have a lock that locked automatically going to her backyard. Then I realized that she, or someone else, would have had to push the little button on the doorknob in in order for it to be locked. The deadbolt didn't lock. Without that button pushed in it wouldn't lock. I tested it. Yep. When you turned the knob it didn't move. There was no way Vera would intentionally do that and step outside. Unless it was pure habit, which seemed unlikely for a patio door.

The only possible way it could have been her was if she truly did it without thinking, and closed the door. Or left the door open and it blew shut. But neither of those explanations gave any reason for her to be outside at night in January anyway.

The patio hadn't been shoveled at all and she didn't have winter boots by the back door, which indicated to me she never used it in winter.

Aware that Pam was going to think I was a freak, I told her, "Would you mind taking a peek at Vera's jewelry and making sure it's all there? Then we can head out."

"Sure. I'll do that real quick."

As soon as she left the kitchen and we heard her going upstairs, I leaned out of the patio door and studied the snow. "Grandma, look at this. This isn't footsteps in the snow. It looks really disturbed."

Snow in January tends to be a little crunchy, not powdery or fluffy. When you walk on it a distinct impression is left behind. So if a little old lady were walking out into snow in high-heel boots, you would see a footprint and tiny holes for the heel. This was a huge swath of snow disturbed, like someone had been dragged across it. Or thrown.

"It looks like she tripped going out the door and tumbled right there. Maybe she broke a hip and couldn't reach the door in time before it swung shut."

It sounded like my grandmother was starting to swing to the accidental death side. Maybe being here was just upsetting her. She looked agitated and pensive. Mortality is not a nebulous concept when you're well into your eighties. I felt contrite. I shouldn't have brought her to Vera's so soon.

"Well, that could be," I conceded. "Come on, we should go before Mom freaks out."

Grandma snorted but she didn't protest.

I took pictures of the patio snow and then the pills on the table.

By the time I had grabbed a few shots, Pam was coming back down the stairs.

"Everything looks fine," she said. "It doesn't look to me like anything has been touched."

"Great, thank you. We're ready to leave."

"Good." Pam handed the key over to me. "If Eva has any questions she knows how to get a hold of me. I guess she and her brother will want to sell this place."

"I really have no idea what their plans are."

We all left and I locked the door behind me.

In the car, Grandma sighed. "This blows."

I cranked the heat. "I know. I'm sorry. 'We only die once, and for such a long time.'" Probably not the wisest time to bust out that quote. I realized that instantly.

"What kind of a smart-ass thing is that to say?" Grandma demanded as I backed out of the driveway.

"It's a quote from a French satirical writer, Molière. It's meant to be funny."

"It's stupid."

"Fair enough." I wrinkled my nose, wishing I could stick my foot in my mouth.

"I want ice cream," Grandma said, sounding like a petulant toddler.

There was a lot to be said against aging. Getting away with throwing tantrums wasn't one of them. I figured you had a right to ask for whatever you wanted when all your friends were dying around you.

"Me too." I was never going to turn down a scoop of vanilla with caramel sauce drizzled over it. "But you have to promise not to tell Mom. She'll kill me if I spoil your dinner."

Grandma moved her thumb and index finger over her lips to indicate they were zipped shut.

I gave her a thumbs-up.

. . .

"RYAN, I'M WAITING," I said as I eyed the spread over my coffee table.

Fried chicken, biscuits, green beans, mashed potatoes, mac and cheese. The works.

I didn't even consider serving it in the kitchen. Ryan couldn't even eat any of it and I needed to relax. That meant I was currently wearing giant fleece pajama pants and an oversized sweatshirt with a sports bra. I had thought about no bra all together but Ryan can be kind of a dirtbag. I don't even know why I own a sports bra. It's not like I work out but, apparently, I had bought it at some point in a moment of pure optimism. It wasn't the level of total comfort I would have preferred but it would do. The fuzzy socks helped and I crossed my legs on the couch, leaning forward to inhale the scent of fried food.

Snagging a bit of the breading off a piece of chicken, I wondered what wine paired best with KFC. There had to be an app for that. Waiting for Ryan I looked it up on my phone.

"Champagne?" I said out loud, reading the suggested pairings. "Get out of here. Fresh, light and modern. Huh. Well, I can do that." I had a reasonably well-stocked wine cabinet and I knew I had a bottle of champagne. I would just stick it in the freezer for ten minutes.

I was closing the freezer door when I realized Ryan was standing on the other side of it. "Geez! I hate how you do that."

"You would think you'd be used to it by now." He gestured to the freezer. "Champagne? Are we toasting my death or the complete disappearance of sexy, youthful Bailey?" He eyeballed my outfit. "I take it no hot date with Marner tonight?"

"I'm relaxing. For your information, though, I don't dress for men. I dress for myself."

He gave a snort. "Right. Stitch that on the sampler in your old-maid house with nine cats."

"There's nothing wrong with a woman who chooses to remain single. Don't be like that." It was a future I wouldn't mind, frankly, if that's the way it played out. "But no, Jake isn't coming over. He doesn't know you are either. He's not sold on one, you being a ghost. Two, our friendship."

"He's jealous of me, even dead." Ryan moved his hands up and down to indicate his body. "Who wouldn't be?"

"He's not jealous." Well. He was kind of jealous. He just didn't understand that having Ryan reappear had brought me peace in knowing that he was okay. It wasn't like I had feelings for Ryan now.

"I'm telling you, he should be."

I rolled my eyes. "Come smell your fried chicken. I'm starving."

Ryan followed me into the living room and sat down with a huge flop. Then he leaned forward and sniffed deeply. "Nice spread. Thanks, Bai."

I picked up a chicken leg and bit it. "So what's this meeting all about, other than fried chicken, friendship, and this day?"

I was still scarred by what had happened exactly a year ago. Hearing that Ryan had committed suicide had been the hardest thing I'd ever dealt with in my entire life. I haven't lost a lot of people and certainly not like that. So sudden and so tragic. Not to mention the fact that I had seen him that day. Oh, and I had tried to kiss him.

The memory of that still made me wince.

"We have an assignment."

Fabulous.

"By the way, did you hear anything about Vera?" I asked. "I'm telling you, she was murdered."

"Can we focus on me for a minute? Is that too much to ask?" Ryan eyed me scooping mac and cheese into my mouth straight from the container. "Also, when was the last time you ate? You look like a contestant at a professional eating contest."

"You're so good for my ego. Not." I went for the green beans. "I skipped lunch today. I just had brunch."

"I'm going to talk and you're going to listen because, seriously, that's a mouthful you have going on there." Ryan looked more amused than disgusted though.

I opened my mouth and showed him my chewed-up food like we were twelve. Ryan brought out the childish in me.

He laughed. "Nice. So here's the deal. I need to tell you this before I get sucked back to purgatory. We have a quota starting February first."

Green beans got caught in my throat and I choked and coughed. I spit the beans into a napkin and looked at him in horror. "What? Why would I have a quota? I'm not on the purgatory payroll. I'm not an ethereal employee. Celestial staff. None of the above. No one has even been in contact with me, which come to think of it is kind of rude. Can I request a meeting? No? Then having a 'quota' can suck it."

"Are you done?" he asked, eyeing me mildly.

Maybe. "And why all of a sudden? I mean, I go my entire life without seeing ghosts, then boom. I'm a medium. I feel like I should have been given a choice. Like, hey, are you feeling helping dead people or is that not your jam?"

"Which would you have chosen?"

"I would have agreed to help you. After that I would have probably opted out. I'm still not over Cesar singing Britney Spears to me at three in the morning."

"I don't think it works that way."

"That's the problem. Neither of us know how this works but now I've been slapped with a quota? On what, by the way?" It occurred to me I didn't even know that.

"Moving spirits on. Maybe you need a class or something," he said. "You're not very good at this."

Insulted, I reached for another piece of chicken. "Am I solving murders or moving people on? Can we get some clarification on that, please?"

"I think they're one and the same. You solve their murder, they move on."

"Which is why I need to solve Vera's murder." See what I did there? Full circle. Boom.

Ryan rubbed his chin. "Maybe there is something to it. So what did you figure out today?"

"The cleaning lady said nothing was stolen. This was on her kitchen table." I pulled out my phone with my free hand and showed him the pictures. "Shoot. I just got chicken grease on my screen. I can't say I really enjoy finger foods." It went against my need for tidiness.

"What kind of pills?" he asked.

"Blood pressure, pain management, sleeping pills."

"So nothing unusual for a ninety-five-year-old. Were there plenty left in each bottle?"

"That I could tell, yes. But look at this." I showed him the picture of her back patio. "It looks like a huge area of snow was disturbed."

"Maybe she fell."

"Maybe she was pushed."

Why did no one believe me? It was seriously frustrating. "Humor me. If she was killed and she is our assignment, what should I do now to investigate? You're the detective here, not me."

"I don't know how a civilian investigates. I would go through her phone and see what was going on right before she died. I would get the phone records to see any deleted texts and check for the GPS. I would see first off, who inherits her estate and how much it's worth. I would check for surveillance cameras in her neighborhood."

"I should have gone through her phone when I was there this afternoon. I have the key now though so I'm going to have to go back and do that." I tossed down my chicken bone and wiped my hands on a napkin. I was done with my fast-food feast. I might have over-bought, something I was known for doing. "I should go back there tonight, before family starts arriving."

"Take Marner with you," he said. "Just in case."

That would go over like a lead balloon. "He's playing poker tonight."

Ryan swore. "I miss poker. This sucks. I'm sick of just hanging around sniffing chicken."

He had never mentioned what had happened in the two months I didn't see him or hear from him and I was too scared to ask. But I didn't think he liked being back in a holding pattern.

"Gambling is a bad habit," I said, because I didn't know what else to say. How do you console a dead person?

He rolled his eyes and did his disappearing act. There one minute, vapor the next.

Clearly he was not feeling great on his death anniversary and I didn't blame him. I wasn't feeling so great about it either. I felt restless and uncertain what to do.

Life felt a little uncertain right now. My parents were on the rocks, my sister was due to have another baby, Jake was turning thirty, his lease on his apartment was up soon. Business was slow, like it always was in the winter, and my best friend, who I relied on to have a shit ton of confidence all the time, seemed down.

It also occurred to me while cleaning up my dinner that part of the reason I was so devastated about Vera was because it reminded me it was possible it could happen to my grandmother. I wasn't ready to deal with losing Grandma Burke. Not now. Probably not ever. But definitely not now.

I HAVE A COMMANDMENT. Thou Shalt Not Leave the House in Pajamas.

So despite how amazing my fleece pants felt, I changed into jeans and a thick sweater to drive back over to Vera's, my bottle of champagne in tow, since I'd never gotten to open it with Ryan and my chicken. I felt like I owed Vera a private toast.

Her townhouse was dark but I flicked a few lights on and looked around. I was kicking myself for not looking for her phone earlier. I went through the whole place and finally found it in her bedroom on the nightstand. It seemed like she had been in bed for the night. There was a water bottle on her nightstand next to her phone, and her covers were pulled back. The TV remote was on the pillow.

I had brought my gloves that allow you to still swipe on a phone screen. Vera didn't have her phone locked, which didn't surprise me. My grandmother didn't either because she didn't have anything on it really. No apps, no credit card info, no bank accounts tied in.

Vera used her phone way more than Grandma Burke. She had social media accounts where she followed fashion and Old Hollywood accounts. She had TMZ. Rent the Runway. Images of sexy men reading books. She had a reading app with hundreds of books on it, from classics to romance novels to modern literature like The Kite Runner.

Her texts were from her friends and her niece, Eva. A man I assumed was her nephew. A couple of guys who were clearly flirting with her. I scrolled through the thread with the man named "Colin" and let out a startled yelp. Right there in their conversation going back and forth, was a dick pic. "Dang, Vera." I quickly scrolled past it, then out of pure curiosity went back because it didn't look like a selfie from a ninety-year-old man.

They say that men don't age *there* the way they do elsewhere but even so... the thighs appeared to be a man in his prime. I suddenly felt like a naughty schoolgirl. Vera might be a cougar, and that was all well and good, but I had a boyfriend.

"Moving on, Bailey." I closed that thread a heartbeat after I should have, and felt guilty as all get-out for that.

Then I found a thread with a man named Stanley.

It appeared he had come into town and had made plans to see her Friday night.

So lovely to see you again, she'd written at midnight on Friday.

Interesting. I wonder if he had any clue she had passed away?

I needed to call him and ask some questions but I needed to work up the courage to do that.

Dashing back downstairs I snagged a crystal flute from her dining room hutch, and using a towel from the kitchen, opened the champagne. I took the bottle and the glass upstairs and poured in Vera's bedroom.

"To you, Vera," I said, glancing around her inner sanctuary. "You were a cool chick who lived life to the fullest. May you rest in peace, dahlin'."

I half-expected her to answer me. Maybe I was hoping she would. But the room remained silent. Vera had a record player on an etagere in the corner and I opened it to see what record was on it. Glenn Miller. I turned it on, not wanting to snoop in silence.

Sipping champagne, I went through Vera's closet, drooling over the vintage pieces nestled up against the modern designers. Nothing was cheap. There were classic, timeless pieces, then funky and fun accessories. She had mastered the art of dressing in well-made basics, then adding shoes, jewelry, a turban, or a funky shawl to change up her look.

Her shoes were to die for.

I gave a laugh of horror in the closet at that thought. To die for. Yikes.

There were drawers lined with felt that had a drool-worthy collection of brooches, bracelets, rings, and necklaces. She even had hairpins that I suspected were from the 1930s. I did notice what looked like some odd empty spots in a few drawers and I wondered how closely Pam had inspected the collection. Or if Pam had swiped a few items on her way out.

There were four stacks of hat boxes, which was glorious.

Beside them were photo boxes. Inside I found newspaper clippings from seventy-five years earlier.

Miss Vera Rosenbaum, 21, model with the House of Chanel, is engaged to legendary film star, Frank Torro, 37. Nuptials to be held at the private home of Humphrey Bogart in a simple ceremony, in accordance with wartime sacrifice.

There was an engagement photo where Vera looked way older than she actually was at the time. Dressed in a suit with shoulder pads, she looked glamourous as hell. Her lips were dark, eyebrows dramatic, hair perfectly curled. Her fiancé was what I would call dapper but not particularly handsome. He was glancing affectionately down at her. On the other hand, she was staring boldly into the camera, sensual and full of life.

"Age is a funny thing, Vera, isn't it?" I said out loud in the closet, draining my glass.

The box was full of old photos. Wedding photos of Vera at different ages. Photo shoots. A three-legged race on the lawn of a mansion, palm trees in the background. Runners laughing as they held on to each other.

Man, I was having a melancholy day.

There were love letters in the box too. Passionate notes from Vera's third husband, things like "Even on the darkest day, you are the sun that warms my soul."

Now it's all text messages.

I would fall over if Marner wrote me a note.

There was also a nasty note from a woman that Vera had kept, which I found fascinating.

It was a woman named June calling Vera a homewrecking whore.

"Why would you save this?" I murmured.

And was June still alive? Had she gotten her final revenge on Vera? That seemed unlikely. She was probably ninety herself.

The record playing cut off suddenly.

I jumped, dropping the letter from angry June.

My heart started racing.

It didn't sound like the record had ended on its own. It had cut off mid-song.

Could Vera do that?

Then I realized I heard footsteps.

Shoot.

Crawling on my belly, I reached the closet door and tried to ease it closed so as not to alert the intruder.

It was too late. I was on my stomach, staring at Italian loafers.

FOUR

GIVEN that the loafers were on the feet of a man who from my position looked enormous and terrifying, I let out a squeak and started scrambling backward. You can imagine how well that worked. I still had the glass flute in my hand, so I was crab walking backward on my wrists. My sweater bunched up to my rib cage and I wondered exactly where the hell I thought I was going. Vera had cashmere, not Kevlar.

I pushed myself up on to my knees, prepared to throw the champagne glass at his chest.

"Are you okay?" the man asked, frowning down at me.

"Who the hell are you?" I demanded, going for offensive. I needed to get out of the closet if I had any chance at escape.

Had I locked the front door behind me? I had to have locked it. I'm obsessed with locks.

"I'm Stanley Robertson. Who are you?" He held a hand out as if to either shake my hand or maybe help me up.

In either case, I ignored it and scrambled to my feet, very grateful I'd changed into jeans out of my pjs. I couldn't die in fleece, that just would not be cool. Stanley had gone out with Vera on Friday night. They'd had a "lovely time." Did he come back on Saturday and bump her off?

"I'm a friend of Vera's." I got to my feet and gestured to the closet, hoping he would enter and I could step out. "Just toasting to her life and her fabulous taste."

"She did have both of those." His voice was easy, his hair trim, overcoat expensive. He had a Burberry scarf on. "As a young gay man growing up in the seventies, she was a fabulous stepmother to have, let me tell you. Despite the quote unquote scandal of her marriage to my father."

Oooh, so this was the stepson Grandma Burke had mentioned. I also knew that one of Vera's husbands had been married when they began a relationship, so clearly that was Stanley's father. Maybe June was his mother of the nastygram. I could see now that he was in his fifties and had either a standing date with a tanning bed or he wasn't a Cleveland resident. He had a deep tan.

I took the chance of stepping forward and it worked. He gracefully moved out of the way. "I'm Bailey Burke," I said. "Vera and my grandmother were very close. I actually took them both to lunch and out shopping yesterday."

He had spoken about Vera in the past tense so he clearly knew she had passed.

"I shouldn't be surprised given her age," he said. "But it still shocked me when Eva called. I just saw her myself on Friday night." He peeled his scarf off. "God, I'm so glad I happened to be in town for work and got one last visit with her."

Stanley was shaking his head and looked genuinely upset. "I'm so sorry," I told him. "I'm sorry to catch you off guard here, too. I didn't realize any family was in town."

He waved his hand in dismissal. "No, it's fine. I didn't tell Eva and Steven I'm here because well, they're not, and I didn't really know them well anyway. Vera was only married to my father for a few years, but it was a critical time for me. She was more fairy godmother, quite literally, than stepmother to the slightly chubby teen gay named Stanley. My father was in denial about my sexual orientation but Vera knew and was completely accepting of me."

He cleared his throat. "She gave me confidence when I didn't have any."

His story touched my heart. "She had enough confidence for all of us," I murmured.

He gave a little laugh. "That she did."

I reached down and swiped up the champagne bottle and my glass. "I was toasting to Vera. Can I get you a glass?"

"Why the hell not?" Stanley said, with a shrug. "I was supposed to be flying home in the morning but now I'm going to stay for the funeral. It's just me and a lovely room at the Ritz tonight."

Because staying at the Ritz must be hell. Not. But I immediately berated myself for the rude thought. He'd just visited Vera and now she was gone. I felt sympathetic toward him.

"Let me put these letters back," I said, handing him the bottle of champagne. "I don't want anything to get messed up."

"Anything juicy?" he asked, with a grin.

"Some love letters, but nothing untoward. Then a nasty letter from a woman named June, who called Vera a homewrecker." I just threw it out there to see if Stanley would react.

He did. His nose wrinkled. "Ah, and that would be my mother. She blamed Vera for my parents' marriage ending, but the way I remember it, it was more from her tendency to go on four-day-long-gin-and-tonic benders with a chaser of cocaine. Dad was a rising music producer and Mom was a fading ingénue."

How very L.A.

"Oh, dear," I said, putting the letters back in the box and closing the lid. "It's a tale as old as time. Man leaves his wife for a younger woman." Though usually minus the cocaine. I think.

"Oh, no, not in this case. It infuriated my mother that Dad left her for Vera, who was in fact, *older* than her."

"Wow." Though I shouldn't be surprised. Vera had it going on.

We went downstairs and into the dining room. I grabbed another glass for Stanley and we sat down at the kitchen table. Vera's pill bottles were still sitting there. I poured the champagne into the two glasses and handed one to Stanley, patting my pocket for my phone. I didn't feel in danger at all but it pays to play it safe.

Though I suppose drinking bubbly with a stranger doesn't constitute playing it safe. I pictured Marner's reaction to this. Lots of sighing and head shaking. Maybe an "Are you insane?" added in for good measure.

"So what brought you by tonight?" I asked him, realizing he hadn't exactly offered an explanation.

"I got the call from Eva this afternoon and I was sitting in my hotel, feeling restless. So I decided to just take a drive to her townhouse, I'm not sure why. But then I saw a light on so I decided to make sure everything was okay. Then I heard Glenn Miller and was totally confused."

"I didn't even hear you unlock the door," I said, fishing a little as I took a tiny sip.

"The door was unlocked."

Weird. That was so not like me. But why on earth would Stanley lie about that?

"So nothing looks odd to you in here?" I asked. "Nothing missing?"

He started. "Why would you ask that?"

I shrugged. "She has a lot of nice things. The housekeeper said nothing was missing but I wasn't sure what with people in and out of the townhouse last night."

"Pam told you that?" Stanley asked, shaking his head and looking disgusted. "I wouldn't trust a word that woman said. I've told Vera for years that she should fire her. I am convinced she was a pill popper." He gestured to the table. "I bet she's the one who left all these bottles here. Vera died, she snagged what she could without it looking too suspicious."

I tried to visualize that. So Pam had come over arguably this morning and stolen pills? It was possible, though if anything she'd just stolen pills that were already out on the table because the cops had told Jake the night before there were pills all over the kitchen and bathroom.

I was starting to wonder if everyone was right and I needed to let this whole homicide angle go. Vera wasn't following me begging me to solve her murder. No one else seemed to think anything was odd about her death.

"How was she Friday night?" I asked Stanley. "Did she seem out of it to you?"

He shook his head. "No. Not at all." He titled his head. "Though, now that I think about it. She did call me Trevor at one point, which was her second husband's name. But I just think that was a random slip-up."

It suddenly occurred to me that Trevor had been the one she'd married twice. The man she had described as the love of her life. I wished I had thought to ask her if she felt now that she presumably had loved all her husbands, and her two fiancés.

Was it possible to love that many men?

I had no clue. So far, I had only loved two, and I wasn't looking to up my numbers any time soon. "How was her marriage to your father, if you don't mind my asking?"

"I need more champagne for that." He poured more into his glass. "They were fire and ice. Oil and water. It was passion and spontaneous trips and smoky nights of jazz. He threw a glass at the fireplace one night and she slapped him for it." Stanley shrugged. "It was a different time, but also, they had that relationship where they loved each other but couldn't live with each other. I think ultimately Vera loved herself more than any of her husbands, to be honest."

Which made her a woman that would inspire all kinds of reactions. Some not so very positive.

"I can't even imagine slapping a man. That is so not me." I also didn't think it was particularly socially acceptable anymore, but maybe I'm wrong. I'm not going to test the theory.

"I'm not volunteering to be your first," he said dryly.

That made me laugh. "I wouldn't dream of it."

"If I'm going to be slapped by anyone it damn well better be a jealous lover."

Hard pass on that. I don't want to either be slapped or have a jealous lover. I like things simple, easy, steady. Which is why being a medium wasn't exactly working out for me. I can't handle the stress of the unpredictable.

I tried to find a tactful way to ask my question. "Is your father still... alive? Did he and Vera keep in touch?"

"My father is still alive but he's in a nursing home. His health is failing quickly. He and Vera have always kept in touch though. It's a fascinating friendship and love."

For some reason my friendship with Ryan popped into my head. Then I instantly dismissed that thought. It wasn't the same. We haven't been lovers.

"I find that very touching," I said.

"Or dysfunctional," he said dryly. "One or the other."

"So what do you do in Los Angeles?" I asked, draining my champagne glass.

"I'm a composer."

"That sounds creative and fulfilling."

"It's definitely rewarding. And you?"

"I'm a home stager with a love of design and fashion. That is part of what I admired about Vera. Impeccable taste."

I suddenly felt like I was on the world's weirdest date. We were heading into odd "get to know you" questions.

"Are you married?" Stanley asked.

That didn't help my feelings of awkwardness. "No. I have a boyfriend," I said. "He's a homicide detective." Maybe hearing I was in bed with law enforcement would make him nervous.

"Sexy. Get those handcuffs out."

Or not.

"If Jake ever handcuffs me it's going to be for my safety, not sexy times. He's all business." Nothing about what I just said even sounded right, or accurate, or anything less than awkward and why the hell was I revealing anything about my relationship to a total stranger? Time to lay off the bubbly.

"I dated a cop once. It all blew up on a weekend in Vegas.

Don't ever let anyone tell you what happens in Vegas stays in Vegas. It doesn't. That shit follows you home and results in an argument where someone gets thrown in the pool."

"I'll keep that in mind." The thought of me and Jake arguing to the point one of us got thrown in the drink made me laugh. That was so not us. "Well, I should probably head home. It's getting late."

I assumed he would leave when I did but he didn't. He stood up and shook my hand. "Pleasure meeting you, Bailey. I imagine I'll see you at the funeral."

"Yes, I'll be there. Nice to meet you even though it was under unfortunate circumstances."

"Indeed."

I wanted to say something else, but I didn't know what. He didn't seem suspicious of Vera's death and why should he? I didn't want to sound like a crazy woman and have my house key to Vera's condo wrestled away from me.

So I let myself out the front door and left.

I hadn't found any life insurance policies or anything obvious to indicate why someone would want her dead, so I wasn't sure where to go from here.

I was sitting in my car, cranking up the heat and shivering, when Vera appeared in the passenger seat. "Oh, geez!" I said, jumping a little. "I wasn't expecting that. How are you, Vera?"

She eyed me with a curious smile. "I wish I'd known you see dead people when I was still alive. It makes you much more interesting than I gave you credit for being."

That was lovely. Being insulted by a dead old lady in designer boots? Check. I could mark that off my life list.

"I'm hoping you mean that way less rude than it sounded."

"Think whatever you want." Vera fussed with the neckline of her nightgown. "Listen, I don't know how much time I have here. But ask your boyfriend what you need to do next."

Because that wasn't cryptic as hell. "Need to do next?" I parroted. "About what?"

"About me. My death. So I can move on." She rolled her eyes like I was a complete idiot.

"Okay." Why would Marner know what I was supposed to do? Did she mean to solve her murder or something else? "Wait. Do you mean Jake or Ryan?" Ryan would know more what to do in the spirit world. In theory.

I thought it was possible she was using the term "boyfriend" just to give me crap.

"Oh, you have two boyfriends? I guess there's a lot more to you than I realized beneath all those freckles."

I barely have freckles at all anymore and what I do have are masked under concealer. That was just insensitive. The glass of champagne had me more mellow than usual otherwise I might have gotten huffy with her.

"I'm just not sure if you're talking about Marner, my alive boyfriend who is a detective, or my best friend, Ryan, who is dead and whose spirit hangs around."

"I didn't even know about your dead boyfriend. That sounds kinky, sweetie, but trust me, no judgment here." She gave me a wink.

I'd never seen Vera without her false eyelashes and she had wispy thin lashes, and non-existent eyebrows. Without her blush and her foundation smoothing out the age spots, and no pop of bright lipstick, it was her eyes that were the most prominent feature on her face. They were dark brown, a rich coffee color, and filled with humor and wisdom. She didn't seem particularly broken up over her death, or confused.

"I meant your living boyfriend. Ask him to figure out what the hell happened to me last night. Because I don't have a clue. It's all like a bad acid trip I took in the sixties. I was in bed and then I thought I heard something downstairs and then I don't know... it's all odd flashes of pills and cold and confusion. And maybe a dog. I swear I heard barking."

I wasn't sure that proved she was murdered, but at the same time, why else would she be sitting in the passenger seat of my car?

I had known it. I'd just known she was murdered and everyone thought I was just imagining a killer.

"I'll do what I can. The local police have no plan on doing an autopsy." Okay, was it weird to mention an autopsy to a dead person? Yikes. But too late. I'd already said it. "I talked to your niece and tried to hint that she might want to order one."

"Who, Eva?" Vera snorted. "Like she would care. All she cares about is getting her grubby little hands on my money."

Interesting. "So you weren't close?"

"Not since her husband made a pass at me."

Now why did that not surprise me? "Did you accept it or reject it?"

Vera glared at me. "What? Of course not! He was married to my niece."

So she drew the line in the sand at stealing family members' husbands but anyone else's was fair game?

"Besides, he was bald. I don't go for bald men."

The truth came out.

"Bruce Willis made bald heads cool for men," I said in defense of all men who were at the mercy of their genetics. "There are some very sexy bald men."

"If you say so." Vera didn't look convinced. "Listen. I need you to fix this, Bailey. I realize death is undignified, but I'm not prepared to spend eternity like this." She gestured to her face, then her nightgown. "That tart in Titanic got to be young and beautiful again when she died. I don't appreciate not getting the same treatment."

"That was a movie. In my experience, you remain as you were when you died. Until you move on. Then I don't know what happens." Hopefully in my case it would be to a seventy-five percent off sale at Saks.

"Then I advise you to die wearing Prada."

"I'll keep that in mind." I turned the heat down in my car now that it was warmed up. "Give me a couple of days and I'll see what I find out, okay?"

"Thanks, I appreciate it. You're a sweet girl."

Or a complete pushover. I wasn't sure which was more accurate.

Vera disappeared and I drove home, suddenly exhausted. Jake called me right as I was ripping off my boots inside my front door. "Hey," I said breathlessly.

"Why do you sound so sexy?" he asked.

"I'm just naturally hot." Nothing was further from the truth but I seemed to have him fooled because he made a growling sound in the back of his throat.

I continued. "I saw your mom today."

He groaned. "Really? You couldn't give me one minute to stay in the gutter? You had to fish me out by mentioning my mother?"

"Sorry," I said lightly, padding in my socks to turn on the table lamp. Not really sorry.

"You can make it up to me."

I rolled my eyes even though he couldn't see me. Maybe because he couldn't see me.

"But yes, I know you saw my mother. She called me after brunch to tell me. She mentioned you're going to go to lunch together to plan my birthday. Please do your best to restrain her. I don't want some huge thing or a surprise or anything like that."

"I know, sweetie. I'll do my best." I poured myself some water. "But your mother is a force of nature and I haven't been in your life long enough to push back too much."

"Your mother is a force of nature. My mother is just Italian."

That made me laugh. "True. But seriously, what am I supposed to say?"

"Say Jake won't want that."

"So she can tell me that I have a lot of nerve telling her what her son wants when she's known you since the womb and I'm your girlfriend of five months? You are very naïve, sir."

He laughed. "Fine. Just make sure that there is alcohol wherever and whatever it is."

"Done. Can you go to Vera's funeral with me? It will probably be Thursday or Friday."

"I have to work but I'll see what I can do. Are you doing okay? How was your grandmother?"

"She's okay. She's with you—thinking I'm imagining homicide where it doesn't exist."

"I never said that. I just said the police's explanation seemed logical."

"So if I was curious enough to, you know, look into it, what would I do?"

"Follow the money. See who gains from her death and if she was planning to change her will or anything like that." He paused. "Just don't go sneaking into sweat baths or going out on dates with serial killers, okay? That's all I ask."

"I would never go on a date with a serial killer now that I'm dating you."

"That's so reassuring," he said dryly. "How are you doing, by the way? Between Ryan's anniversary and Vera? Do you want me to come over?"

I pulled the leftover chicken out of the fridge and bit a hunk off of a thigh. "Nah, I'm okay, but thanks though. I appreciate that."

"What are you eating?"

"Fried chicken."

He didn't say anything for a heartbeat. "Sometimes I wonder who exactly I'm in love with."

"I'm a mystery." I didn't actually believe that but Vera would encourage me to keep the aura of mystique going.

"Totally."

"I'll talk to you tomorrow," I said, wanting to eat my chicken in front of my laptop. "I love you."

"Love you too."

I meant to do research on Vera's life but I only got as far as discovering her condo was valued at $612,000 on Zillow before I got sucked into a design show on HGTV. What was the obsession with granite, anyway? And we all know popcorn ceilings are clearly the devil. That's just a given. Thirty minutes later, I was dozing off from the crazy weekend, the poultry, and the champagne.

My phone ringing jerked me awake. Startled, I sat straight up, heart thumping. It was almost midnight. Phone calls that late are always bad news. I felt sick. Was it Grandma Burke? Had the stress of Vera's death given her a heart attack?

It was a heart attack.

But not Grandma Burke.

It was my mother.

FIVE

JAKE BROUGHT me a cup of coffee the next morning in the waiting room. We'd spent the night on the hard seats of the emergency room lobby for six hours, my father sitting next to me in total stunned silence. They had just reassured us that Mom was going to be fine. They were transferring her to cardiology but she would most likely be released in a few days after they assessed how much damage, if any, had been done.

I was exhausted from worry, my eyes swollen from crying. My sister in Texas was blowing up my phone all night and all I had been able to tell her was that we didn't know anything yet. All we'd really known was that she was alive, which when I first heard my father's voice breaking on the phone the night before, I had been uncertain of for a split second.

Jake sat down next to me and took my hand in his. He'd insisted on picking me up and driving me to the hospital when I had called him hysterical the night before. He hadn't wanted me driving and he'd been right. I couldn't have seen through my tears.

My mother is a force of nature, just like Jake had said. She has a conviction rate of ninety percent as a prosecutor and is well-known for taking cases other prosecutors wouldn't touch if she believes in someone's guilt. She's headstrong, brilliant, and a little bitchy. Her maternal instincts are crap, but her court instincts are fantastic.

I had always assumed she would live to a hundred years old, criticizing everyone all day long. The thought that she might be *gone,* in a split-second, had tilted my world on its axis.

And good Lord, what if her ghost came to me afterwards? The thought froze all my blood to ice.

I gave the sign of the cross and thanked God she was still alive.

The coffee took some of the fog off of my brain and I turned to my father. "You should go home and get some rest."

He just shook his head. "Once they move her upstairs, I'll head to her room. I want to see her."

That touched me. My parents had their crap but they did love each other.

"It shouldn't be long."

It wasn't. After five minutes had passed, they told us we could go upstairs. Jake insisted on waiting in the hallway and letting me and Dad go in alone. Grandma was at home. I would have to go get her later and bring her for a visit. My mother looked pale and fragile but fully with it. She was telling the nurse attending her that she was doing her job wrong.

"You should put that on the left side. Then you wouldn't have to pull all this tubing across me."

The nurse made a noncommittal sound. Give the poor girl three days and she'd be contemplating pulling the plug.

"Hey, pumpkin," my dad said. He squeezed my mother's leg but made no move to get any closer to her. He looked like he was afraid he would break her.

"Hi, Mom, how are you feeling?" I asked, standing awkwardly at the bottom of her bed. Mom isn't a hugger.

"I'm fine. You didn't need to come all the way out here. I don't want to be responsible for those bags you have under your eyes."

And... now what. This was the way it always was with her. You tried to be nice and she repelled you like a roach with a jumbo-sized can of Raid. "You had a heart attack, Mom. Of course I'm here."

"Bailey, can you step out of the room? I want to tell your father privately that I want a divorce."

The nurse bumped into the metal cart and medical equipment rattled.

I stared at my mother. "What?" One, what? Two, how was saying she wanted to tell him privately but then stating it anyway actually private? And three, what?

She ignored me and turned to my father. "I could have died tonight and I realized I'm miserable. We're miserable. Life is too short. I know about Judy and this is pointless."

"Who the hell is Judy?" I squeaked, astonished and feeling like I might vomit.

The nurse was studiously looking down, frantically trying to finish her job so she could bolt. I couldn't blame her. I wanted to bolt right along with her. Maybe to the locked closet where they kept the knockout drugs. What the hell was happening?

"This isn't the time," my father told her, sounding nervous, and guilty as hell, I might add. "You've had a scare. Just relax. We'll revisit this particular issue in a few days and see if we can come to a resolution that works for both of us."

"Don't corporate-talk me," she snapped.

"I think we should wrap up visiting time," the nurse said. "Mrs. Burke, I need you to stay calm."

"This is insane," I told them both.

"Mind your own business," my father said sharply to me.

And... I was out. Only my family could turn a heart attack into a farce. I felt like I'd fallen into an episode of Supernatural because clearly my mother had been possessed by demons.

"Mom, I'll call you later. I love you."

I ignored my father, who obviously had a girlfriend named Judy.

My mother waved to me but didn't say anything.

"Um..." Jake said, when I went into the hallway, not sure whether to cry or laugh.

"My mom is fine," I said flatly.

"I heard. I heard everything, unfortunately."

"What was that?" I asked him. "She's lost her mind. Though my father apparently already did that a while ago since he didn't deny the Judy accusation." That made tears pool in my eyes. "Oh my God, my father is a cheater. That's so gross."

He was holding my coffee and he took a huge sip. "Babe, let's not jump to any conclusions. It's been a long night. Maybe your dad just didn't want to argue with her eight hours after she had a heart attack."

That could be true. I took a deep breath. "Honestly, I wouldn't even care if they got divorced. It's their life and they're not exactly the poster children for marital bliss. But I don't want my dad to be having an affair."

He put his hand on the small of my back and rubbed as we walked down the hallway. "Let's just wait for the facts. But yeah, that wouldn't thrill me about my father either."

"Promise me if you ever fall out of love with me or you're tempted to be with someone, that you dump me, okay?" I shot him an earnest look and took my coffee back out of his hand.

Another guy would have spent the next ten minutes outlining why he wouldn't fall out of love with me or cheat, but what I like about Jake is he knows what I need and that was not it. I needed exactly what I had asked for.

He nodded. "I promise, Bailey."

The cold air smacked me in the face as we stepped out into the parking lot. I shivered. "Let's run away to Florida."

"You don't have to ask me twice."

I wondered if ghosts would leave me alone in the Sunshine State.

"That would be a negative," Ryan said, sliding across the ice in his work boots.

I wasn't even sure how he was doing that given he wasn't actually solid. It seemed he'd learned acting skill since his death.

"Sorry about your mom."

I gave him a slight nod. I did not need a weird pissing match between him and Jake right now.

Vera appeared beside Ryan, walking in her cheetah boots.

My life was an acid trip gone wrong.

"Can we go to your apartment?" I asked Jake. Ryan had never gone there. I didn't know why, but it seemed like a bro code thing. "It's closer and I need to sleep for about nine days."

I shot both my ghostly hang-abouts a warning look.

They both blinked at me innocently, like they would never interrupt me sleeping or during anything else. "What?" Vera asked. "I can take a hint."

I slipped on the ice and would have gone down if Jake hadn't managed to grab my arm at the last minute. Why did I have the distinct impression that Vera had pushed me?

She had never struck me as malicious but she was no angel either.

Though she shouldn't be able to touch me.

Most likely I was just a klutz.

"We should have planned a beach vacation," I told Jake. "I'm over this already and it's only mid-January."

"We can go away for my birthday in March," he said, sounding hopeful. "By then we'll really be ready for sunshine and then I can avoid a party."

"I say yes to this plan." I needed something to look forward to. Or maybe just to distract me from what had just happened. "But I think it's highly unlikely you'll be able to escape the party."

"The good with the bad," he said. "That's life."

It sure was.

WHAT A WEEKEND FROM HELL. Jake only slept two hours before going to work. I stayed in his bed until noon, unable to shake sleep or fogginess. I had gotten little sleep all weekend and had been busy shopping and brunching and dealing with Vera's death and Ryan's death anniversary. Then bam, my mother's heart attack and announcement. Craziness.

I had a massive headache and my face felt like someone had jammed cotton up my nose and punched me in the eyes a couple of times. I was scared to look in the mirror, knowing I was going to have a red nose and swollen lids. Not that I had any intention of going anywhere. I had already canceled my work appointments for the day, explaining my family emergency. I was wearing Jake's T-shirt and pajama pants and I was still going to be wearing them when he came home from work.

After noticing that my super adorable boyfriend had made coffee for me, but it was long cold, I pulled out my phone and used UberEats to get myself a latte the size of my head and a bagel loaded with schmear.

Jake had texted me twice, one a little kiss emoji, the other a simple "Are you okay?" My sister, Jen, had called me five times but I honestly wasn't sure I could handle her right now. Alyssa had called me three times and had texted me. Apparently, Jake had told her what had happened and he wanted her to check on me. Did he think I couldn't be left alone with the knives or something?

First I texted him so he would stop worrying.

I live in your pajamas now.

Then I texted again. *I'm okay, thanks. Xo.*

"What the hell is going on?" Alyssa demanded when I called her.

"My mother had a heart attack and then told my father she wanted a divorce." I flopped on Jake's couch. "She told him she knows about Judy and life is too short to be miserable."

"What the hell?" she repeated. "Who is Judy?"

"I have no idea but my father didn't deny it. The doctor told us my mother will be fine but they're keeping her at least a day or two for tests and observation." I knew I had to call her and my father but I didn't really want to. I had no clue what to say.

"Damn. On the heels of Vera. What a shit weekend."

"For sure."

"Are you at home or Jake's?"

"Jake's."

"Okay. I was going to come over after work and hang out with you but if you're with Jake that's cool."

"You can come over here, you know. He's not a territorial boyfriend. He knows I have friends." I never wanted to be perceived as that kind of woman—who chose her boyfriend over her friends or who couldn't still have her own life.

"I'll bring wine. I try not to drink on weeknights but if ever there was a Monday made for wine, this is it."

"Truer words were never spoken. Okay, I have to go. I really need to call my parents and my sister. I just woke up."

"Got it. I'll text you later."

We ended our call and I got a text saying my food had arrived. I went downstairs to the front door of Jake's duplex and grabbed my coffee and brown bag of food. I could tell the guy was trying not to judge me for being in pajamas and looking like a zombie snatching that coffee like it was brains, but he didn't entirely succeed. "I work nights," I told him, which absolutely shocked me. I'm not one to lie normally but it just popped out.

I wondered if I was in violation of my No Pajamas in Public commandment. I was in semi-public, so it was shaky ground. The look on his face said he agreed, which irritated me. I see people in pajamas all the time.

He just nodded and told me to have a good afternoon. Maybe he could care less about what I was wearing and I was just hypersensitive from being exhausted and stressed. I drank the coffee even as I walked back up the stairs, dribbling some on my chin, hoping I hadn't closed the door all the way or I would be locked out.

The door had swung shut on its own. Damn it all to freaking hell. I *was* locked out. Jake didn't have a spare key lying around. He was a cop and he would never do that. I jumped up and down in irritated frustration before realizing at least I was still holding my phone. I ordered Lyft and five minutes later I was on my way home, to where I did foolishly have a key hidden in my garden by the back door. If I had thought the guy bringing my food had questioned my outfit, I can't even imagine what the driver thought about me being in socks in January with six inches of snow on the ground. I had no coat, just an oversized T-shirt and flannel pants. I shivered in the back seat and clutched my hot coffee.

He kept glancing at me in the rearview mirror.

"I got locked out," I told him. "I ordered food and forgot to take my key downstairs with me."

"Oh," he said. "Gotcha. Want me to crank up the heat?"

"If you don't mind, thanks." My feet were wet and icy cold. My fingers were numb.

How did people live here before central heat and cars? Coldly, obviously.

Ten minutes later I was dashing down my driveway as fast as I could, flinging open the gate to the backyard and bouncing on the balls of my feet as I tried to lift the fake rock containing my key out from under the bird bath. Easier said than done since it was covered in snow and frozen to the ground. I gave several choice swear words as my red, wet hands slipped off of it. Finally, I figured I could just open it without lifting it off the ground.

I had no feeling in my fingers but somehow I managed the task.

"Only you," Ryan said, appearing next to me. "Seriously. Only you."

"Thanks for the support," I said, teeth chattering. My hair was falling forward, so I swiped it back as I finally gripped the key and stood up. The wind blew Jake's T-shirt close against my chest.

"Holy nipples," Ryan said.

Really? I was in a T-shirt and it was twenty-five degrees outside. What did he expect? "Pervert." I blew on my fingers and ran up the back steps. It took me three tries with my frozen digits but I opened the back door and stumbled in, thanking God and my furnace.

I grabbed my puffy coat off a hook by the back door and immediately sat down at the kitchen table. I pulled the coat on and then reached down and yanked my wet socks off. I zipped the coat and flipped the hood up before standing again and shoving my coffee in the microwave to get it piping hot again. What a Monday to go with my crap weekend.

The only upside was the cold had reduced the swelling in my face from crying.

"What happened to you?" he asked.

"I got locked out of Jake's when I went downstairs to get my food delivery."

His eyebrows shot up. "Why didn't you just call him?"

"Because that's not the world's dumbest thing. Sure, leave work to come home to let your idiot girlfriend in. Everyone at the station thinks I'm a nutcase as it is."

"That's true."

I rolled my eyes. "Besides, what was I going to do, stand in the unheated vestibule in my socks? I figured this was easier, which it would have been if it were July." I took my coffee back out after the microwave stopped and took a sip, burning the roof of my mouth but not caring. "Now excuse me while I go get some socks."

I decided as I sat on my bed and pulled on my fuzziest fuzzy socks, that in order to avoid thinking about my family, I was going to do some research on Vera. I did text my father and my sister just to touch base but neither answered me right away, making me think they might actually be on the phone with each other. Thank goodness.

Trading the puffy coat for a tank top and a sweatshirt, I went back downstairs and opened the bag with my bagel. That went in the microwave next. Ryan was sitting on the couch, boots on my coffee table.

"I'm going to research Vera," I told him. "You know, follow the money. See who might want her dead. Her condo is worth over six hundred thousand but I don't know if she owns it outright or what.

Also, her former stepson seemed to think her niece is a money-grubber."

"Isn't everyone?"

"No. You never were."

"True. You can't take it with you. You can't even take a change of clothes with you."

That was a seriously depressing thought. "Vera is none too happy about that."

"None of us are happy about it."

I pictured Cesar in his swim trunks sitting on my couch. Yeah. None of us were happy about it.

Two hours later, I had hit a wall in research. I had put Vera into Google and I found all the basics. Her social media, property transfers, those old articles about her marriages. Nothing particularly noteworthy.

Then I got something. "Hey, Vera sued her nephew, Steven. Wow. Who does that?" I scanned the details of the lawsuit. "It's actually a countersuit. He sued her for her portion of his father's estate, saying she was mentally unsound. She sued back alleging fraud."

Ryan was asleep on the couch next to me. Or resting his eyes. He didn't respond. I snapped my fingers in front of his face. "Wake up."

"Huh, what?" He pretended to wake up.

Being dead must be seriously boring if these were the ways he needed to entertain himself.

"Vera's nephew sued her for his father's inheritance. Or her portion anyway. What kind of guy does that?"

"A greedy one."

"It was a million dollars. I guess that's a decent incentive."

"When was this?"

"Five years ago. Steven lost. There was no basis to say Vera couldn't handle her finances. Which I totally agree with."

"Who inherits from Vera?"

"Presumably her niece and nephew, so he's going to get the

money in the end. I doubt she spent much of it. So what was the big deal?"

"He must have needed the cash. Though who is hard up when they've just had a mil dropped in their bank account? I'd check that guy out. Maybe he's heavily in debt. Five years gone by now he's probably run through the original inheritance and figures he can't hold out until Vera dies a natural death. It's possible. Though doesn't he live somewhere else?"

"New York."

"So now we're assuming hit man? That's a stretch."

"Couldn't he drive here, kill her, and drive back?"

"With CTC footage and electronic toll passes? Seems stupid."

"Not if no one is going to think it's murder," I pointed out.

"You're reaching."

"My only suspects are the housekeeper, the niece, and the nephew."

"I vote housekeeper."

"This isn't an election."

"It should be. Then we could meet our quota."

Ugh. "Don't bring that quota crap up to me. I can't handle that today."

My phone rang. "Oh God, it's my father." The thought of talking to him made me sick, but I needed to hear how my mother was doing. I put the phone to my ear. "Hello?"

"It's Dad."

I loved how my father still assumed I didn't know who was calling. "Hi, how's Mom doing?"

"She's fine. Something about putting her on blood pressure medication. No real damage to the heart. Doc told her she needs to reduce her stress."

My chest tightened. "I'm glad she's okay. But how is she supposed to reduce her stress unless she retires? Would she even consider that?"

"No, of course not. She's only fifty-eight. She wants another five years in. She would die of boredom if she was retired."

"Yeah, but her health." I knew it was a futile protest. My mother was happiest working, putting bad guys behind bars. She wouldn't enjoy retirement, he was right.

"Listen, about what she said."

Please, no, please don't, I chanted in my head.

"I don't know how serious your mother is about a divorce but I'll do whatever she wants me to do."

What did that even mean? "Okay. And Judy?" I asked, because I couldn't stop myself.

"Is a friend. Nothing more."

I suddenly remembered where I'd heard the name Judy. She was the wife in a couple my parents were friends with. She'd gotten a boob job and her husband had gotten a boat and Grandma said Judy spent all summer wearing tank tops without a bra. My mother had thought she was ridiculous. Obviously not the reaction my father had. I sighed.

"Dad. You can lie to me. That's fine, because ultimately, it's none of my business, though I have to say I would be incredibly disappointed if you cheated. But whatever you do, don't lie to Mom. No one can lie to Mom and get away with it."

There was a pause, then all he said was, "You're right. It's none of your business."

Good talk. "What do you want me to do? Should I go see Mom or just wait until she gets home?"

"Truthfully, I would wait until she gets home. She's a little frustrated with the hospital setting."

No shocker there.

In some families it would be considered horrible not to go visit someone in the hospital but that wasn't my mother. She couldn't stand to be fussed over or seen as weak. If she said don't show up, she meant it. It wasn't a platitude. "Okay. But I will call her."

"Great. I'll talk to you soon."

"Bye."

I ended the call and sighed, shoving my laptop computer off

my legs. "My father is having an affair with a woman who got a boob job. How cliché. I thought he was better than that, seriously."

It depressed me no end. I picked at the remnants of my bagel and stood up. I wanted the rest of that fried chicken.

"Men struggle to face their own mortality," Ryan told me, sounding like Dr. Phil.

"Don't give me that crap. Oooh, I'm afraid to die so let me bury my face in silicone?" I rolled my eyes. "Excuses. It's called boredom. Thirty-five years with someone, just out the window because you wanted to order off a different menu."

Ryan held his hands up. "Don't look at me. I probably was/am incapable of monogamy. I know that about myself."

That was why it was a good thing we had never been more than friends. "How charming."

"Listen," he said, suddenly sounding contrite. "I'm sorry about your parents' relationship, but everyone makes mistakes, Bai. Everyone. It's not our place to judge anyone else."

I paused in front of the fridge, my anger deflated. Ryan was right. He had lived that way when he was alive. I had no business judging my father when I didn't even know the full story. What happened in a marriage was known only to the two people in it.

Plus possibly Grandma Burke. She lived with them and is nosy as hell.

"You're right."

Ryan pretended to slam dunk. "I love being right."

"Then help me solve Vera's murder."

"Blah, blah, blah."

Just like that, every good feeling toward him evaporated.

My phone rang with an unknown number. Normally I wouldn't answer that for all the money in Vera's bank account.

But now I was saved from murdering a dead man. "Hello?"

"Bailey, it's Stanley. I got your number from Vera's phone. I'm bored and bereft. Will you meet me downtown tonight for drinks?"

I really wanted to stay in Marner's pajamas but this was a

perfect opportunity to get more information about the will. "Sure, if my friend Alyssa can join us. We already had plans."

"The more the merrier. I'll call you later and we can have pretentious cocktails."

"As opposed to plebeian cocktails?"

He laughed. "Exactly."

When I ended the call, Ryan was frowning. "Who was that?"

"Stanley, Vera's stepson."

"He sounds like a dick."

"So much for not judging people." I bit a piece of chicken. "You need to go soon. I have to shower and get ready."

"Leave the shower on for me. I want to see if I can feel the water."

"You can't."

"How do you know? You suck as a medium."

I got close to him and blew on his face. "Do you feel that?"

"No. And don't do that. It's weird."

"What's weird is my life."

SIX

"I CAN'T BELIEVE you want drinks downtown today of all days," Alyssa said. "It usually takes you a crane to get you downtown."

That wasn't totally true. "Only when you want to go to a club. I'm too old for clubs."

"You're twenty-eight! By thirty-five you'll be eating dinner at four p.m. if you keep this pace up."

That was a slight exaggeration. But not much. "I do get hungry early. In fact, I'm going to have to order an appetizer before I even have a drink. It's after six."

She shook her head and crossed her legs, showing off gorgeous over-the-knee boots that somehow looked more glamorous than dominatrix. She was also wearing a velvet circle skirt in defiance of the weather. Stanley wasn't due to arrive until seven but I needed to eat and wanted to hang out with Alyssa alone before he arrived.

We were at a cozy upscale bar that served cocktails with airplane-themed names. "I'm going to have the First Class. After I have a charcuterie board."

"I want the Mile High."

"Of course you do," I said, grinning at her.

"It's the only thing close to action I'm getting these days."

"Are you okay?" I asked her. "You still seem down."

She waved her hand. "We are not going to talk about me and my ridiculous screwing myself over by revenge-dating a dick I then started to like. It's just stupid. You're the one who needs sympathy. Your mom and dad... wow. I don't even know what to say."

"Ryan told me I just need to let it go. That I don't have a right to judge my dad. Or my mom for that matter."

Alyssa's eyebrows shot up. "You just said Ryan instead of Jake. Oh my God, Bailey. That is so not good." She looked at me like I had bought a house in Loserville.

Alyssa doesn't know I see ghosts. So, yeah, that was mortifying.

I decided it was now or never to come clean. I flagged down the bartender. Might as well get my drink order in first before my BFF declared me insane. "I'll have the First Class cocktail."

"Excellent choice."

Anything with booze in it was probably a good choice today, but sure. Let's go with excellent choice.

"You, miss?" he asked Alyssa, his eyes briefly dipping toward her cleavage.

"There's nothing there for you," she told him.

He laughed. "Sorry."

When he moved away, Alyssa confronted me. "You're seriously not even going to respond to the fact that you referred to your boyfriend, Jake, by your dead crush's name?"

"I wasn't talking about Jake," I told her. "I can see Ryan. As a ghost. He first showed up last August and has sporadically been around since then."

I pretty much just blurted it out but I wasn't sure there was actually any other way to drop news like that.

Her jaw dropped. She reached for her phone and started swiping.

"What are you doing?" I asked. "Aren't *you* going to say anything now?"

"I'm on Google looking up if stress can cause hallucinations."

I put my hand over hers to stop her frantic swiping. "Stop. I'm not hallucinating. Ghosts are real. And I see them."

"I am speechless. You've made me, the loudest bigmouth you know, speechless." She sipped her water. "Where the hell is my cocktail?"

"I know you're not sold on the concept of the paranormal. I wasn't either. But I can't deny that ghosts exist and they like to hang around me. It's annoying, but oddly comforting. I didn't tell you because I thought you'd think I was crazy."

Alyssa wasn't saying anything, just pursing her lips like she was trying to prevent a torrent of "Are you insane?" flying out of her mouth.

"Jake saw Ryan slam a door shut."

"Jake sees ghosts too?"

"No. But when I told him I do he wanted some kind of proof. So I had Ryan slam the door shut. I think he reluctantly believes me."

"Ryan hangs around here and there? That's not awkward or anything." The bartender was going to set her drink on the counter but she just demanded, "Give that to me," and took a huge fortifying sip.

His eyebrows shot up.

"Jake isn't thrilled about it."

"You're basically in a ménage."

The bartender paused in the middle of setting my drink down. He couldn't quite mask his intrigue.

"I am not! Ryan knows not to show up when I'm with Jake." That didn't sound exactly right either. "Ryan and I are friends. Nothing more."

"This is so weird."

"Tell me about it." When the bartender finally moved out of earshot, I lowered my voice. "I can see Vera too. And twice I saw Hannah, Ryan's girlfriend."

"Holy shit."

"Tell me about it. Vera told me she wished she had known when she was alive that I see ghosts because it would have made me more interesting."

"That sounds like something Vera would say, I'm not going to lie."

"Exactly." I took a tiny sip of my drink. I needed my cheese board before I really got going on it. "The thing is, only murder victims show themselves to me, so that means Vera was murdered."

"Who would kill a ninety-five-year-old woman? That seems like wasted energy. It's not like she had another twenty years."

"That's what makes it odd, yes." My best friend seemed to be taking the news that I was a medium reasonably well. "The most obvious reason would be someone wanted her money."

"Or her wardrobe. The bitch was stylin'."

"Agreed." My cheese board arrived and I started noshing on it. "Are you okay with all this ghost stuff? I don't want you suddenly avoiding me because you think I'm a freak."

"Oh, I still think you're a freak but that has nothing to do with you seeing ghosts." She gave me a grin. "I don't know what I believe but who am I to say it's not possible? Two hundred years ago no one even knew bacteria and viruses exist. Maybe we haven't evolved enough scientifically yet to explain other dimensions."

That was an interesting way to consider it. "Very true. When you start to really dissect it, science itself is almost unbelievable. Fantastical."

"I wouldn't say unbelievable. It's provable data. Now. But I am open to considering the possibility of ghosts, just skeptical. Mostly I find it ironic that it would be you they're showing themselves to."

"I know. That is ridiculous, isn't it? Because, let's be honest, I am not a goth girl or a hippie."

"No, you're Laura Ashley."

I was hoping more like Donna Karan but okay. I could see the floral reference.

Stanley came into the bar, his nose red, suit jacket inadequate for the weather. He did have his Burberry scarf on but that would protect two inches of your neck and no more. His California mentality wasn't going to cut it in Cleveland.

"Order me a hot toddy," he said, pulling out the stool next to me. "And a ticket to Turks and Caicos."

"I can do the drink. The plane ticket you're on your own."

He leaned over and air kissed me as I waved for the bartender. I loved the way he had instantly declared us friends.

"Stanley, this is Alyssa, my best friend. Alyssa, Stanley, Vera's stepson."

She held her hand out toward him and he took it. "Well, aren't you gorgeous?"

Boom. Alyssa liked Stanley. She smiled. "Why, thank you, handsome."

It wasn't flirting. I'd given her the heads-up about Stanley's orientation. Alyssa loved to both give and receive compliments. I'd had a feeling they would enjoy each other's company.

"I need a gin the size of my head," Stanley said.

After we exchanged casual conversation along the lines of "lousy weather" and "did you get your flight changed?" Alyssa took charge of the conversation.

"Do you believe in ghosts?" she asked Stanley.

I jerked, my feet hitting the bar in front of me. Seriously? I shot her a warning look, which she thoroughly ignored.

Stanley seemed to think it was an odd segue into the evening. Which is was. "Is there a reason for that question?"

"Bailey just told me she sees ghosts."

What the hell? "Alyssa. I told you that in confidence."

She genuinely looked surprised. "Oh, you did? You didn't say that."

"What do you think? Do I seem like the kind of person who wants to be known as the kooky medium? I don't even own any incense."

She snorted. "One of my favorite things about you is how fast you leap to the absurd. Okay, sorry, I didn't mean to spill the spiritual beans. Scratch that, Stanley. Forget I brought it up. You're sworn to secrecy."

"I clearly walked in at a bad time," he said, flagging down the bartender.

"Cheese, Stanley?" I asked him, indicating the brie on the board. "It's delicious."

"Ah, the favorite way to change the subject. Cut the cheese." He gave me a humorous look.

I laughed. "When you put it that way... I feel like I need to clarify." I didn't want him to think I was seeking attention.

There were plenty of legitimate mediums, and I genuinely believed in that, well before Ryan had shown up in my kitchen at the crack of dawn. But there were also a ton of frauds who either liked the attention or the cash and I was mortified at the idea that anyone might think that of me. That was really why I was compelled to be silent. I didn't want anyone to think I could be faking it for some kind of material or emotional gain, because one, that's not the kind of person I am. Two, I would throw this back if I could.

So far I had no out.

In fact, I now had quotas. (Yes, I am still bitter about that.)

"I had a very close friend who passed away and eight months after his death, he appeared to me." See, that sounded super innocuous. Like no big deal.

"That's fascinating. Why do you think he appeared to you as opposed to say, his mother?"

"I don't know. I think it has to do with the fact that he wanted me to solve his murder."

His eyebrows shot up. "A post-death request for justice. How very 'Ghost' of him. Is he as hot as Patrick Swayze?"

"Yes," I said.

"No," Alyssa said.

Stanley laughed. "To each her own, huh?"

"What are you talking about?" I asked Alyssa, offended on Ryan's behalf. "Ryan was attractive."

"There's attractive and then there is Patrick Swayze hot. Stanley said Patrick Swayze hot and I took that very literally. I mean, any of his roles he was just so sexy it's a shock movie screens didn't burst into flames. Johnny, Darry, and whoever the hell he was in Road House. Ghost. *Hot*. With Ryan it was more like 'congratulations on your face, you're not ugly.' He didn't have that secret sauce that Patrick did." She shrugged. "I mean, no offense to Ryan."

I sipped my drink, waiting for her to keep talking, because she certainly seemed to be enjoying it. "Are you finished presenting your dissertation?"

"Yes." She looked to Stanley. "You get what I'm saying, right?"

"I absolutely get what you're saying. It's the same with Paul Newman. You could leave me alone with that man's corpse, and I'm not sure I could be trusted."

Alyssa cackled in amusement while Stanley grinned that she'd found him funny.

"The minute I saw your dark hair I knew you were as wicked as me. I love it," Stanley said.

I was just sipping my First Class and feeling horrified. I got it wasn't *literal*, but ew.

Then again, no one called me Funny Girl.

"Gross," I said, and they both just laughed harder.

"So what have we established here?" Stanley said, after taking his drink from the bartender with a wink. "Besides the fact that Alyssa and I don't give a shit about being PC and Bailey either dreamed her dead ex out of sheer trauma or she did, in fact, see his attractive, but not secret sauce, ghost."

I felt like I was on a date with my boyfriend and the girl who within a week was going to replace me. They were just feeling each other and it was annoying. No one wants to introduce two people she likes to each other and then feel like they both like each other more than they like you. I was Jennifer Aniston with Brad Pitt and Alyssa was Angelina Jolie.

I popped a piece of cheese in my mouth, very sorry I had even so much as mentioned ghosts to Alyssa. Or invited Stanley along on our girl time.

"We should leave her alone," Alyssa said, as if I were a super-sensitive child they were teasing. "She's had a rough weekend."

"I don't need a nap," I said. "I need you to believe that I am not delusional or still in love with Ryan."

"Still? That's very telling," Stanley said. "Tell me more."

I was frustrated and I took a deep breath. "No. That's not want I meant. Just forget I said anything. Let's talk about something else entirely, like, Stanley, why were you in Cleveland to begin with? I don't think you ever said."

"I think you need another drink, Bailey," Alyssa said, sounding sympathetic. "You sound tense."

Oh, now she was worried about my feelings? I love Alyssa, but she loves an audience. She was playing to the audience, i.e., Stanley.

I felt beyond irritated.

"I'm here on business," Stanley said, in the world's most generic answer. "Pop in, pop out."

"That's what he said," Alyssa said.

"I knew you were going to say that. I just knew it."

"Hey, you handed me that. You wanted the cheese, admit it."

"Guilty. Who doesn't love an overplayed sexual innuendo?"

I shifted back so they could fawn over each other with a more direct sightline.

"Excuse me," I said, pushing my stool back.

It was tempting to just grab my coat and walk out the door but this wasn't a bad date. It was my best friend and Vera's stepson. But I wasn't going to settle in and spend the next four hours with them either.

The restroom was thankfully empty so I could splash water on my face, heated from emotion.

I half expected a ghost to appear next to me. It seemed like the perfect moment to irritate me further, but no one floated in beside me.

Determined to not be a rag, I took a deep breath, attempted to tame my wild curls, and touched up my lipstick.

Then I went back with a smile.

"What the hell?" Stanley was saying. "My cuff link is missing. Did I drop it in my martini?" He peered down into his mostly empty glass.

"What does it look like?" Alyssa asked.

That seemed a pointless question since a cuff link was a cuff link but Alyssa sounded a little tipsy.

"It looks like a cuff link," he said.

I glanced down at the floor but there didn't seem to be anything small and shiny flashing up at me. "I don't see it anywhere."

"Oh, well, it wasn't my favorite set anyway. For all I know I swallowed it."

"I guess you'll know tomorrow," Alyssa said.

Stanley frowned. "That's rather crass."

She frowned. "Oh, really?"

Uh-oh. Their instant attraction might be wearing thin. There can't be two centers-of-attention.

I'm ashamed to say that made me feel a hell of a lot better.

VERA'S FUNERAL was an odd assemblage of random people, from a group of Hassidic Jews to a trio of drag queens, wearing full-on stage makeup and costuming, despite it being ten in the morning. According to Eva, Vera had always said she didn't want a religious funeral, so it was just held at the funeral home, with a reception at the country club afterward. The parade of people into the room was immense and fascinating. The only demographic that seemed to be missing was children.

Not Vera's thing, that was for sure. She had made it very clear she'd never regretted not having kids.

My father was bringing Grandma Burke and Jake had managed to leave work long enough to meet me there.

"This is quite the crowd," he said, looking around at Team Vera. "There are a lot of men here."

"Vera liked men."

One man in his forties was weeping openly. I wondered if he was a relative until I heard his female companion call him Colin. Oh, geez. This was dick pic Colin. My cheeks bloomed with heat.

Don't picture it. Don't picture it.

I pictured it.

Oh my God, I was picturing *that* at a funeral. At least we weren't in church. That would ensure my seat on the bus to hell.

A woman came over to us. "Are you Bailey?" she asked. "I'm Eva."

"Oh yes, it's nice to meet you." I eyed the niece, trying not to be too obvious in my assessment.

She didn't look like Vera. She wasn't as striking, and she had a round face, which was surrounded by a halo of brittle bleached hair. It wasn't blond. It was the caramel color that happens when brunettes with very dark hair try to go blonde and can't get all the black to leech out before the stylist drops the blond on.

"What a ridiculous display of drama," Eva said, rolling her eyes as Colin walked past her crying. "And how utterly trashy of a man who was blatantly taking advantage of an old woman for money. Disgusting."

I wasn't sure that anyone had ever taken advantage of Vera in her entire life but I wasn't going to argue with Eva about it. "Vera was a sugar mama?"

"Of course. What fifty-year-old man wants an old bag otherwise? My brother said she bought him a car. It's just so tacky that he's even here."

Interesting. Note to self: investigate Colin as more than just a lover. Is he a gold digger?

"Is this your husband?" Eva asked, eyeing Jake in a way that suggested she didn't quite understand the meaning of the word "tacky."

"My boyfriend. This is Jake."

Yep. She was full-on leering. "You're a lucky girl."

I shifted closer to him and looped my arm around his elbow, suddenly afraid she might try to hug him. "I know."

"Oh, there's Pam," Eva said. "Unbelievable. I can't believe she would have the nerve to show up here."

Apparently, a lot of people had a lot of nerve today.

She moved away, probably to confront Pam. On the way, she handed a tissue to Colin and snapped, "Pull yourself together."

"She's something," Jake said. "Though I'm not sure what."

"Amen to that. I wonder where her brother is," I murmured. If he was anything like Eva, I wanted to avoid him.

Without warning, there was the sound of voices raised in anger coming from the lobby.

"Get out of my face!" we heard quite distinctly.

Every head in the room turned to see what the ruckus was about.

It was Pam, the housekeeper, backing up and waving her hand in Eva's face.

"Oh, dang," I murmured. "This can't be good."

"Should I go break it up?" Jake asked. "Deescalate the situation?"

"I'm not sure that's possible, but maybe we should try to do something."

Now Eva had lunged at Pam and was grappling at her wrist. "Give me that, you thief."

"Get off of me, bitch!" Pam yelled right back.

There were gasps in the room and I jumped up, following Jake, who was already moving down the aisle to the lobby.

"What is going on here?" Jake asked. "Why don't we step outside and talk this out."

He tried to herd them toward the door but they were having none of it. They totally ignored him.

"I have every right to be here," Pam said. "Vera was good to me and I was good to her. I considered her my friend, not just my employer, you crazy hag."

Eva made a sound in the back of her throat that was more

angry cat than grieving woman. I didn't think I would want to go up against her, to be totally honest. "Oh, please," she said. "You were stealing both pills and money from her. And now you've stolen her bracelet." She gestured to Pam's wrist.

"She gave this to me months ago."

I wasn't sure I believed that.

Jake was blocking them from the view of the main room but he interjected here again. "Ladies, this isn't the time or the place. Come on, opposite sides of the room." He touched Pam's elbow and steered her to the left.

She went easily enough, sniffing a little. But Eva shocked the hell out of me by making a dive at Pam's wrist. She ended up getting a grip on her coat sleeve and yanking Pam backwards.

Pam was either a female wrestler in a prior life or no stranger to girl-on-girl crime because after she recovered from her stumble, she turned and went for Eva. She had her down on the ground before Jake hauled her off of the screaming Eva.

I had no idea what to do other than to stand there in horror. I did offer to help Eva off the floor but she waved me off and hauled herself to her feet, wincing. Then she tried to rush Pam again.

In theory, I could step in front of her to prevent further confrontation. In reality, I was scared to be squished in a Pam and Eva sandwich. So I just let Jake turn Pam and block Eva with his body. I mean, he's a cop and I'm a home stager so let's just stay in our lanes.

Besides, by this point people were rushing over to help. One of the drag queens stepped in front of Eva and said, "Honey, just calm your tits."

My sentiments exactly.

Eva drew up short, which was understandable. The guy was well over six feet tall and had a flawless complexion and smoky eyes that were to die for. If I wasn't mistaken, he was wearing Louboutins with a six-inch heel that had him a towering mass of faux fur and leather leggings. I felt like I had as a little girl seeing

Cher perform on TV—in awe of this man's sheer coolness and confidence and no cares to give about anyone's opinion.

Everyone seemed to settle down and both women were being talked down off their crazy ledge.

I realized when I turned slightly Vera was standing next to me.

"Now that was awesome," she said, giving me a grin. "Who else gets to witness a fist fight at their funeral?"

"As long as you're happy," I said quietly, figuring in all the melee no one would notice I was talking to myself.

"Very. This is a good turnout. Oh, and for the record, Pam did steal that bracelet. I haven't seen it in months. Eva may be a bitch, but this time she's right."

Interesting. So Pam was a thief and a liar. Was she a killer too?

"Poor Colin," Vera said, glancing around the room. "Those tears are genuine, I believe. He was very enamored of me."

Then she actually wandered away from me, which had me shaking my head. I was pretty sure she couldn't actually be present there if I wasn't there, and yet she was blowing me off?

Not that I cared though. It's hard to have a conversation with a dead person no one else can see.

It was her funeral. I guess she wanted to mingle, check out the mourners.

Eva and Pam had been ushered to opposite sides of the room and were sitting down.

Jake shook his head at me like he couldn't believe what the hell he'd just seen and reached out for my hand so we could go resume our seats.

I spotted Grandma Burke shuffling in at the last minute, looking annoyed. My father wasn't known for being punctual. My father also looked like he might have had a pre-funeral cocktail.

Fabulous.

I spaced out when the funeral director, or whoever he was, was speaking but once mourners came forward to give speeches about Vera, I paid closer attention.

Making notes in my phone of the names of people who seemed

over-the-top, which was nearly everyone, I didn't even notice Jake was watching me.

He leaned over and put his lips close to my ear. "What are you doing?"

"Making notes." I showed him my screen.

COLIN- LOVER, seems to be taking it too hard (acting?)
Pam- thief
Eva- greedy
Steven- MIA (where is the nephew??)
John- her next-door neighbor, could have locked her out

JAKE'S EYEBROWS rose but he didn't say anything else. I realized if he had noticed maybe someone else had too and thought I was casually surfing Twitter during a funeral. We were almost in the front of the room. Everyone who chose to speak had to walk past me to get to the podium. I slipped my phone in my pocket and prepared to make mental notes.

After the ceremony, I did discretely (though probably totally noticeable to anyone, let's be honest) checked the cards on all the floral arrangements that had been sent. Lots of names I didn't recognize. But there was one from a Richard Robertson, who I had to assume was Stanley's father, given the card said "All my love always."

Stanley had said he was very ill, so he clearly couldn't travel for the funeral, but had still wanted to offer his sympathy. I thought that was really sweet. That years and years later, after their relationship had ended he still cared about her. Now that was a talent —inspiring life-long devotion.

There were flowers from Colin and flowers from the rabbi and his wife. Other than that, I didn't really know the majority of the mourners' names.

The whole experiment was a bit of a letdown.

It wasn't until Jake and I were driving home that I reached into my pocket for my phone.

It wasn't there.

"Jake, where's my phone?" I asked, frantically plumbing the depths of both of my pockets.

"I don't know. You put it in your pocket."

"Turn around!" I felt all around the seat of the car, the floor, even checked my purse though I was certain I'd put the phone in my pocket. "It must have fallen out at the funeral home."

"Let me call it first." Jake was already turning around though. He knew me well enough to know I don't misplace things. "Call Bailey," he said to his phone.

No ringing.

Also, I wasn't sure I was glad or disappointed I wasn't in his phone by a cutsie nickname.

At the funeral room, the director let us look around but we didn't find my phone. There were only a few stragglers left and they were heading toward the door.

"This sucks," I said to Jake. "I don't see how it could have fallen out."

I had a sneaking suspicion that someone had stolen it. Like Pam, who had hugged me.

Did she see me making notes? Did she think I was on to her or was she truly just a common thief? Thank goodness my phone was password protected.

"Use the app on your computer at home to find its location. It's probably here, just kicked under a chair. The cleaning crew might find it."

"Of course," I said, though I didn't believe it at all.

I was starting to become a conspiracy theorist. This is what seeing ghosts had done to me.

SEVEN

"I GOT YOU A PRESENT," Alyssa said three days later as she blew in to the coffee shop and dropped a brown bag on the table in front of me.

"Is this in sympathy for the fact that my parents are nuts?"

My mother had come home from the hospital the day before only to immediately hire movers and start packing. She wanted me to go with her on Saturday to see some condos she was interested in buying.

My father, not to be outdone, had gone on a three-day bender at home that had resulted in a DUI when he tried to leave the house for more booze, only to take out the neighbor's mailbox, who called the cops. He had then booked himself a trip to Florida for the following week to play golf. With Judy.

"No, you get no sympathy from me on parents having midlife meltdowns. My mother bought a farm and went off the grid when she caught my dad cheating, remember? Your mom is just buying a lakefront condo. You'll have access to the marina restaurant and the private beach if she chooses wisely. All I got was a chance to pet goats, who are way cuter on YouTube than in person."

I sipped my coffee and reflected on that. "Fair enough."

"Three days later and I'm still in awe of that shitshow that was

Vera's funeral. Who attacks someone over a bracelet? That was straight out of reality TV. Real Housewives style."

I still wasn't over losing (aka someone stole it, I freaking know it) my phone. "Vera would have loved it."

"True." She shook her head. "That's the way I want to go out. A million years old in Saint Laurent, with people being ridiculously overdramatic at my funeral."

Sipping my coffee, I eyed Alyssa's outfit of the day. According to my friend, it was never too early for oxblood-colored lipstick. She had on double eyelash extensions and had her hair in a very high ponytail with curls and prominent bangs. Her sweater was bright green and a second skin. I was pretty sure she was going to make an impression anywhere she went.

"I think if you stay the course, you can have your wish." I fingered the bag she had set down. "Can I open this?"

"Of course."

Inside was a book on learning how to become a medium. I raised my eyebrows at her. "Does this mean you believe me?"

"Like I said, I don't believe or disbelieve. But if you're going to have ghosts hanging around you, it can't be all amateur hour up in here. Learn your trade. Figure out how to control it. Otherwise it has the potential to wreck your life."

I thumbed through a few pages, not really reading much beyond the headlines. "You are one hundred percent right. I should have looked into this months ago. But I was kind of hoping it would go away."

"I've learned burying your head in the sand and wishing something will go away never works."

My new phone rang with an unknown number. Given business had been slow lately, I went ahead and answered it.

"Is this Bailey Burke?"

"Yes, it is."

"This is Jonathon Simms, attorney for the late Vera Rosenbaum's estate. You were named in her will."

My jaw dropped. "What? Are you serious? What did she leave

me?" God, I hoped it was a handbag. Just one. I'm not greedy. Preferably Chanel.

"She left you five thousand dollars and a handbag." There was shuffling. "Hermes."

Holy crap. "Oh my God," I blurted. Either one of those would be a huge gift, but both? I was flabbergasted. "That was very generous of her. I'm in shock."

"I think she would take great joy in hearing that," he said, a little dryly. "Vera had a blast setting this will up. She left five grand to fifty different people."

That was so Vera. Spread the wealth. Give a little sunshine to a lot of people. "Wow, I'm super grateful she thought of me. She was a very fascinating woman."

He gave me a few more details and I ended the call.

"What?" Alyssa asked, impatient. "What was that?"

"Vera left me five grand and an Hermes handbag."

"Holy handbag!"

Alyssa's phone rang.

"That's the lawyer's number! Answer it."

"Hello? This is Alyssa Dembowski."

She listened for a few seconds, eyes growing wide. She gave me a thumbs up. "That's amazing, thank you. I'm really touched."

After a few more "uh-huhs" and "thanks" Alyssa hung up the phone. "I got five grand and her mink coat. What the hell, Vera? She rocks."

"Can you imagine just doing that? Giving money to fifty different people?"

"*Fifty?*"

I nodded. "That's what he told me. She left fifty different people five grand."

"Well, I don't feel quite as special now, but I'm not complaining."

"Me either. I imagine the only people complaining this morning are her niece and nephew. This had to dent their inheritance."

Alyssa waved her hand in dismissal. "Screw them. What did they do to earn the right to her money? Be born to her sibling, that's it. It doesn't sound like either of them even saw her in years. I hate when people think they're entitled to an inheritance. When I die, I'm doing a Vera and I'm going to tell everyone. I don't want my kids circling my carcass like vultures." She sipped her coffee. "You know how evil people are. How many sixty-year-old kids have helped Mom and Dad along quicker than nature intended? Oops, Mom took a spill. Dad accidentally over-dosed on pain meds. You know it happens."

"Sadly, I'm sure it does." That's why I was suspicious about Vera's death. Maybe if she had let her family know they weren't entitled to everything she had, she might still be alive.

"That's why I'm making it clear to my kids they aren't getting jack-squat so they don't bump me off when I'm helpless."

"I hope I don't give birth to selfish children, but I guess it's luck of the draw."

"Some people are born assholes. It's just a fact."

"Let's not ruin this moment thinking about our future children murdering us."

Alyssa nodded. "Maybe I just shouldn't have kids. I don't want to sleep with one eye open."

That made me laugh. "Paranoid, much?"

"It pays to be cautious."

My phone rang. "My grandmother is calling me. I bet she got money too." I swiped at the screen. "Hi, Grandma."

"I just got a call from a lawyer. Vera left me five thousand smackers. Isn't that something?"

"She left me five grand too."

"What? Well, heck. Now I don't feel so special."

The same reaction as Alyssa. I rolled my eyes.

"But that's good," Grandma continued. "You should set it aside for your wedding."

"What wedding? Isn't Dad supposed to pay for that?" I didn't really believe that my father was obligated to foot the bill for my wedding but it seemed like a good deflection from an unexpectedly awkward conversation. "I already have a house and a business. I'm going to go on vacation with some of the money and save the rest. Jake and I want to go to Florida." I also might want to buy a pair of shoes to go with the handbag Vera had left me, but she didn't need to know that.

"Florida? What's in Florida?"

I swear my grandmother said things just to start crap. "Beaches. Sunshine. Margaritas."

"Don't get pregnant."

Oh God. "I have a handle on it."

"I hear that sponge works well."

And... now I wanted to die. "Thanks. I'll keep that in mind. Listen, I wanted to talk to you about what you're going to do now that my mom is moving out. Do you think you'll be okay staying there with just Dad?" She was my father's mother but he was not only having a love affair with Judy, he was in bed with gin most nights. I wasn't sure how safe it was for her there.

"Your mother suggested I move in with her but that sounds like hell. It was nice of her to offer, though."

That actually surprised me. "That was nice."

"I'd kill her. Or she'd kill me. The only thing that prevents that now is this house is enormous and most of her anger is directed at your father. I don't want to be the solo target."

"Good point." I wanted to offer for her to come and live with me but I have a lot of stairs. Plus, I felt like I needed to talk it through with Jake, get his temperature on the whole situation since I was pretty sure he'd been hinting around that we should move in together. "I'll talk to Dad. But I think you should stay with me next week when he goes on his golfing trip. Mom needs to rest."

That made Grandma snort. "Sure. Your mom resting. That's hilarious. But yes, I would love to stay with you, Margaret. Thanks for asking."

"It will be fun. We can do our nails and watch romantic comedies. Hey, how was your date?"

"I canceled. Turns out he was making moves on Shirley too."

"I'm sorry." Relieved. I was relieved. I didn't think I could handle Grandma staying with me and needing a ride to meet up with a beau.

"Easy come, easy go."

After our goodbyes I ended the call. "Grandma is pissed that she wasn't the only one to get money from Vera."

"I feel that, I told you. Are you really going to Florida with Jake?"

"Hell yeah. I don't know when we're supposed to get this money. I imagine it will take months but that's what my credit card is for. This weather is nasty. I need sunshine."

"That idea has merit."

"My grandmother told me not to get pregnant."

Alyssa laughed. "Why would you get pregnant in Florida as opposed to say, Tuesday here?"

"I have no idea." I lifted my mostly empty mug. "Do you need a refill? I'm going up."

"I'm good."

The coffee shop, a local chain, as opposed to a conglomerate, was crazy busy as usual. They served vegan pastries and eco-friendly coffee, whatever that means exactly. I was waiting in the line three people deep, absentmindedly looking around at the art for sale on the walls when I realized a man was staring at me.

I quickly glanced away, as you do when you accidentally make eye contact.

Then I looked back, because he looked very familiar. Maybe he was the husband of a client of mine?

This time he looked away when we made eye contact. Maybe I was wrong and I didn't know him at all.

But as I was walking back to the table several minutes later with my overly full mug, it hit me. I'd seen him at Vera's funeral.

"Alyssa," I hissed. "Look at that guy over there. The one in the burgundy sweater. Wasn't he at Vera's funeral?"

She looked up from her phone and glanced around. "What guy? And so what if he was? It's a popular coffee shop."

Frustrated, I tried to turn discreetly, but we've already established I suck at discreet. "He's right there," I said, gesturing slightly. "By the sugar and honey station. He's around forty, in shape, tight sweater. Gray hair."

"I don't see him. Is he a ghost?" she said, though by the tone of her voice it was a joke.

"How can you not see him?" I asked, frustrated. But when I turned back I saw she wasn't really making much of an effort to look. She was shopping for shoes on her phone, probably with the inheritance from Vera.

"I know he was there," I said stubbornly.

"So are you suggesting he's following us? Or you? As opposed to the very realistic possibility that he just wanted a latte?"

"I've been followed before," I reminded her. "And the guy hit me with a car."

That made her glance up, looking contrite. "That is true. But what are the odds that would happen twice?"

"I don't know but I'm not crossing the street until he's gone."

Easy for her to be dismissive. She hadn't sailed through the air and bit it on asphalt.

"If you really want to be safe, you should leave first then. It's just logical."

"Fine." I shoved my coffee at her. "Thanks for the book. I'll talk to you later."

I grabbed my coat and got the hell out of there before Tight Sweater Man tried to shiv me with a fork.

"ARE YOU SERIOUS?" Jake asked. "Because if you are, I'll put in for vacation days tomorrow."

"I am very serious. I'd say as a heart attack but that's too close to home right now." We were sitting on Jake's couch after eating a dinner of flank steak, asparagus, and red potatoes that he had cooked for us. I was pleasantly full and slightly less stressed than I had been in the past week. "When do you think you could get off of work?"

"March is probably not going to fly." Jake was sipping a glass of whiskey, his feet up on his coffee table. "All the detectives with kids want off for spring break vacations. I bet I can get off in February though."

"The sooner, the better. Where should we go?" I lifted my wine glass to my lips and sighed, picturing a balcony overlooking the ocean and me in a floral print cover-up. I wouldn't object to three days of seeing my boyfriend shirtless on the beach either.

"Can we go to Key West? I've always wanted to go there."

That was a very Jake response. Live music and cheap beer were right up his alley.

"Is there a beach there?" I asked, not really sure. I'd never been to Key West either.

"There has to be a beach there. It's Florida and it's right on the water."

"As long as there's a beach I'm happy." I reached over for a blanket from the arm of the couch. I was freaking freezing as usual.

"Where were you thinking?"

"I don't know. Ft. Lauderdale. Ft. Meyers. Something with a Ft. in it."

"We can go to Ft. Lauderdale if that's what you want." He reached for my hand and lifted it to his mouth. He kissed the back of my hand. "Ladies choice."

"Let me think about it. I mean, no matter what, it will be awesome. It's free money and it's an escape from scraping ice off my car windows. It's a win."

"Whatever you want, sweetheart." He tugged at my arm. "Why are you so far away? Come closer."

"Why don't you come closer?" I asked.

"Because if I go over there, what am I going to do, lay on you? I'll crush you. If you come over here, you can lay on me, which I happen to really enjoy anyway. So it's a win." He gave me a charming, mischievous smile.

I couldn't resist that smile even if I was perfectly cozy under a throw with my wine in hand. I set the glass down and shimmied over to him. "So... how serious are you about me having whatever I want?"

"Is this something kinky? Then yes."

I smacked his arm as I cuddled onto his chest. "What? No. Ew."

Jake laughed. "Why ew? What are you even thinking I'm thinking?"

"I don't know! No, I mean do you love me enough that if I say something might need to happen that you probably won't like, will you be okay with it?"

As I gazed up at him, he barely moved a muscle. Jake was reliable in that he would never freak out on me or get angry. The only indication he was even concerned was the little dent that appeared between his eyebrows. "There is no way for me to even answer that convoluted question, Bailey. But yes, I love you. Yes, I am willing to compromise and deal with unpleasant situations in life. I think I've proved that."

He was right. "You have. You totally have."

"So just tell me what's going on."

"You know my mom is going to a condo. I know her well enough to know this isn't something she'll change her mind on. She's decisive and never flakey."

"Agreed, from what I've seen, yes. I know you're upset about your parents and I'm sorry about that. I'll help in whatever way I can. Does she need me to move furniture or something?"

I wish it was that simple. "No, she'll just hire someone. She likes to pay people because it's easier than to be demanding."

Jake gave a laugh. "The suspense is killing me then."

"Dad is drinking way too much and suddenly planning golf trips with his paramour. Grandma Burke is his mother and, honestly, I don't think it's safe for her to be living with him anymore and I can't stomach the thought of assisted living for her. Not yet, anyway. Maybe in a year or two."

"Oh God." He gave a hearty sigh. "You want her to live with you, don't you?"

I gritted my teeth and gave a tentative, "Yes? What do you think? Am I crazy?" I held my breath. His opinion and comfort mattered to me.

"No, you're not crazy. She's your grandmother and your family is going through a huge upheaval. If you really think she's not safe with your dad then you should consider it."

Best. Boyfriend. Ever. He was so freaking mature he made me feel like a tween sometimes when I got bratty. I was a lucky lady. "I would have to move my office upstairs so she would have a first-floor bedroom."

"True. Do you think she'd miss her friends and her parish? She's pretty involved in church."

I hadn't really thought that far ahead. "I guess she would. But it would be better than assisted living, right?"

"I think anyone her age would agree with that, yes." He took a sip of his whiskey.

"Our privacy would be seriously compromised." Unfortunately compromised. *Grossly* compromised.

He nodded. "It would. But it wouldn't be forever, right? And your grandmother is one, hilarious. Two, pretty damn deaf."

That made me laugh. Then I had a sobering thought. "Yes, but I won't ever be able to stay over here at your place."

For a second he didn't say anything and my neck was developing a serious crick staring up at him in anticipation.

But then he just came right out and said it, because Jake does that, unlike me, who beats around the bush for an hour. "I could move in with you. My lease is up in April."

Holy big step. My face went hot and I felt like I'd swallowed a lemon. But at the same time, it seemed so... right. Apparently, my worry about why he wasn't staying over as much was for naught.

He wanted to *live* with me. Permanently. "You, me, and Grandma?" I asked.

"Why not? I wasn't expecting the third party but moving in together was already on my mind."

Because he was mature. I wasn't so sure about me. I opened my mouth, not even entirely sure what was going to come out of it. "I think that sounds perfect."

It did. Whoa.

"Really?" He looked surprised by my answer. But he pulled me tighter in against him. "That's awesome. It's going to be awesome."

"We're going to scandalize your mother," I said.

"I'm almost thirty years old. My mother will recover. Plus, we'll have an eighty-five-year-old chaperone."

He was kissing me when I felt a cold draft behind me.

"Aw. How sweet. Lovebirds shacking up."

It was Ryan, being Ryan.

But I completely, one hundred percent ignored him. This moment was all Jake.

EIGHT

OKAY, so my concern over Vera's death had gotten a little shuttered due to my mother's heart attack, my parents' divorce, and Marner and me agreeing to live together. With my grandmother.

Jake swore his mother was fine with it, but I wasn't holding my breath on that. No phone call from her for dinner plans to plan his birthday, by the way, so I had a feeling she was reeling and needed time to process cohabitation before marriage.

Neither of my parents gave a rat's ass that I planned to live with Jake. Actually, that's not entirely true. My mother supported it as financially sensible. My father didn't care much either way other than I think he recognized it got him off the hook for odd jobs around my house. He also really liked Marner. They were both football and fishing fans.

Grandma Burke wasn't sold.

"That's not the way we did it in my day," she said, after I picked her up the next week to stay with me during Dad's vacation. "You got married first, then you bought a house and moved in together."

"I know, but times change. We're in a committed relationship."

"So, then what's the issue? Just get married."

"Yeah, why don't you just get married?" Ryan asked with a grin, appearing in the back seat.

Grandma turned to Ryan, not the least bit disturbed that a dead guy had just hopped a ride. "This is a private conversation, young man," she said.

That made me snort. "No conversation is ever private when you see ghosts. You should know that."

"It's rude."

"Sorry, Mrs. Burke. I was just trying to back you up. About Bailey's sinning with Marner and all. I mean, living together and not getting married?" He gave a low whistle.

Hilarious. He was just so hilarious. I needed to change the subject.

"Grandma, Ryan says I have a quota. I need to solve a certain number of murders a month."

"Well, that's a corker," she said. "Seems a little difficult to manage that. Who gave the order? Because if it came from the big guy you have to take it serious." She made the sign of the cross. "Otherwise I'd negotiate."

I assumed by "big guy" she meant God, but I didn't want to ask specifics. "I'll look into it."

"So how's it going so far this month?" she asked.

I made a buzzer sound. "Nothing. The only murder I'm aware of is Vera's and I haven't figured anything out with that. Plenty of suspects but no evidence."

"Where did the money lead you?" Ryan asked.

I was driving but I glanced at him in the rearview mirror then realized that his reflection was much weaker that way. He was almost vaporous. It was a startling reminder that he wasn't actually alive. Which I knew but this was a weird kick in the teeth.

Putting my uncomfortable thoughts aside, I gave a shrug. "Vera left five grand to fifty people. I'm not sure about the rest of the details of the will. I assume her personal possessions she didn't designate in the will go to her niece and nephew, along with her condo."

"Oh, didn't I tell you?" Grandma piped up. "That lawyer told me Vera left the condo to me."

I swiveled my head so hard I felt my car float to the right. I corrected my driving but then glanced quickly at my grandmother. "What? That condo is worth six hundred thousand dollars!" Maybe Vera had it mortgaged to the hilt but I doubted it.

"Is it? I never knew that. But there was a note for me with the will. Vera wrote that she was leaving it to me so I would be more independent."

What the what? That was just crazy. Sure, they were good friends, but that was a lot of real estate. Though it sounded like Vera had plenty of cash and little affection for her niece and nephew. "Why didn't you tell me this the other day?"

"It slipped my mind. I had no intention of moving in there. I don't want to live alone."

I didn't want Grandma Burke living alone either. "That's fine, but we need to sell it or rent it or something. It needs to be dealt with. How are Eva and Steven supposed to get her stuff out of there? Or actually, is it the lawyer who catalogues that stuff? Since I'm guessing all fifty people in her will were given a personal item as well."

"Beats me. Talk to the lawyer. I'm just an old lady. I still have a flip phone."

That amused me. "That's not even true. You have an iPhone. You should consider getting an Alexa too."

"And have that woman listen in on everything I'm doing? Forget it."

Because my grandmother was doing so many furtive and scandalous things? But I guess that wasn't the point. "You think Big Brother is watching you?"

"Somebody is listening to those things. Probably robots, but still. Privacy is privacy."

I wouldn't know what privacy was any more since I had ghosts dropping in like spiders and Grandma moving in with me.

Speaking of intrusive entities.

"You're not doing a very good job investigating this case," Ryan commented.

"I've been busy!" Seriously busy.

"Not working. Yesterday you were shopping online for new furniture while watching some British baking show."

Okay, that was true. But to be fair to me, I needed to furnish Grandma's new bedroom. "I was shopping for work. I am a home stager, if you recall."

Just the thought of my business, "Put It Where?" made my shoulders shoot up to my ears. Business was slow and here I was planning a vacation to Florida and moving my grandmother in with me. Brilliant strategy. Not.

A thought occurred to me. "Wait. How do you know what I was doing? I didn't talk to you yesterday."

"I didn't want to interrupt you."

"Ew. Don't stalk me, you weirdo." I pulled into my driveway and put the car in park. I looked back at him. "Seriously. Don't do that."

Ryan's normal grin was completely missing. "Then get on it, Bai. *Seriously*. There's a lot riding on this."

The tone of his voice unnerved me. He sounded angry. Or maybe just tense. "What do you mean?"

"What do you think?" He just shook his head. "This isn't a joke to me. This is being stuck with no control, no power, nowhere to go. No *life*. Don't you get that?"

I was stunned. Of course I got that. But how could I really understand it? I couldn't. I felt a flush of heat in my cheeks, ashamed that I was annoyed with his showing up unannounced when in reality I could do whatever I wanted with my days. Ryan couldn't.

"I'm sorry. You're right. I have pushed this aside. I didn't realize how much it meant to you."

I had been busy with personal circumstances but that wasn't fair to Ryan. Or Vera.

"It means everything."

Nodding, I said, "Got it. What should I do? Start talking to people close to Vera?"

"Call the boy toy," Grandma said. "He's shady."

It wasn't like I thought Colin was going to confess to me, but I figured if I made him nervous, he might slip up and do something stupid to implicate himself. "I can do that."

"See if there is CTC footage going in and out of Vera's condo complex. If she was shoved outside, someone had to go through those gates. It's gated, right?"

"Yes." I should have thought of that. Though why the hell anyone would let me, the home stager, see that footage was beyond me. I needed to cook up a lie. Pretend to be a relative.

"Look into the bingo girls too. There was some bad blood a few months back," Grandma said.

"Vera played bingo? That seems so out of character for her."

"Oh, she didn't play to win, she just played for the gossip and the man-hunting."

I had my hand on the door handle to open it but that gave me pause. "Women man-hunt at bingo?"

"At my age, women hunt for men everywhere. The odds aren't in our favor."

"I would have thought bingo guys were too old for Vera."

"This conversation is making me uncomfortable," Ryan said. "Can we not talk about the old lady's love life?"

"Old people make whoopee, kiddo. I hate to break it to you," Grandma said.

I love the term whoopee. I think we need to bring it back.

"I never said they don't. I just don't want to talk about it."

Ryan was clearly in a mood today.

"Do you know the bingo ladies?" I asked Grandma, attempting to regain a modicum of control.

"Yes. I introduced her to them."

"Oh." That made sense. "Were they at the funeral?"

"Of course. Bad blood doesn't change that."

"When is the next bingo session? We should go."

"It's Friday. I'm in."

Jake was going to love me for that. We were supposed to go play darts on Friday night. Not that he should mind. I was basically a liability to him anyway. Initially I had fallen for the idea of being a couple competing together against other couples, but the reality is I have noodle arms with zero aim. I've hit everything from the wall above the dart board to the bartender. Don't worry, he wasn't seriously injured. Just a nick on the forearm. Jake's pride was more damaged than anything. His cop friends all have sporty girlfriends, which is so not me.

I got out of the car and went around to help my grandmother. The driveway was icy as usual and her bones were like onion strings.

It was a good thing I wasn't working much (yeah, right) because I had a ton of phone calls to make. I got Grandma in the house and settled in watching ancient episodes of Touched By An Angel and started working the lines.

First I called Eva, playing the sympathy card. I assumed she was back in Florida, but I wasn't sure.

"How are you doing?" I asked, injecting concern into my voice. "I heard about the will."

Eva clearly needed to rant so she didn't even seem to think it was odd that I was calling her. "Isn't that just insane? I mean, what was Vera thinking? My God, she basically gave money to people off the street. Now I'm just debating if we chalk it all up to her being mean-spirited and let it go or pursue legal recourse."

Mean-spirited? So, Eva thought it was mean-spirited to generously gift fifty people with money? I suppose she meant mean-spirited to keep it from her and her brother. "Surely she left you something," I said, trying to gain more information.

"We got the life insurance but that was only three hundred thousand. Split in two after taxes that doesn't add up to much. We're basically both out an additional five hundred thousand between the condo and the money she just tossed around. Not to mention all her personal assets. She had some quality jewelry and handbags, as you know. She only gave me a dozen items."

I'm not sure what world Eva lived in that a hundred and fifty thousand dollars "didn't add up to much." The majority of the population would probably disagree with her but clearly she was ticked off to be receiving way less than anticipated. "Did you decide to do an autopsy?"

Now I was really being ballsy but what did I have to lose? She was a thousand miles away from me and presumably couldn't harm me. Plus she was very loose-lipped.

"I asked for a very basic autopsy. Toxicity report, primarily. I think we're going to find she had a stroke or overdid her medication. She was really too old to be living alone, you know."

Maybe. I also suspected it had never dawned on Eva to have Vera go live with her in Florida. "It will be nice to have closure," I said.

"Also, if it proves she had a stroke say, months ago, we can contest the will."

Nice angle. I wondered if it was a red flag that Eva was so open about her greediness. No killer would be so open about her desire for money, would she? Or maybe she thought it just made more sense to be honest? No. I was pretty sure I could eliminate her from my suspect list. Her brother I couldn't reach any conclusions yet, but Eva had been in Florida and wasn't even attempting to hide her desire for Vera's cash and possessions.

It took another ten minutes of listening to her complain before I could get off the phone. I decided that calling Colin was way too aggressive. I had no angle, no reason to call him. Instead, I figured he was probably using social media. Maybe I could establish an alibi for the night Vera died. Eva had given me Colin's last name so I started searching various sites and apps.

Within a few minutes I clearly saw that on that Saturday Colin had been busy all through the evening and late at night. He'd gone to dinner downtown with three friends, then to a comedy club, and later, on to a trendy bar geared toward customers in their forties and fifties. Colin seemed to have a lively social life, with lots of friends. Every weekend he was doing something. Antique shopping, dinner and drinks, the theater.

Given the timestamps on his posts, with GPS marking the location, I didn't see how he could have killed Vera, unless he'd gone over there at 2 a.m. and somehow convinced her to get out of bed and go outside. That seemed far-fetched.

Who did that leave me? I pulled my blanket tighter around me as I sat at the kitchen table.

It seemed like it only left Pam, the housekeeper, and Steven, the nephew.

Or someone yet unknown.

Not one of the bingo ladies. They were all Grandma's age and half didn't even drive anywhere. Besides, there was no motivation other than revenge for a falling out and that seemed far-fetched.

If this were the sixties, I imagined I could come up with lots of enemies who might have wanted to kill Vera, but now? It didn't seem like a lot.

Though it did occur to me that if someone in the will knew they were getting five grand, desperate times might call for desperate measures. Eva had said it was basically people off the street and maybe it was. Maybe it was handymen, the neighbor, her personal shopper at Saks. Who knew?

The will opened up a suspect list fifty people deep.

Well. Forty-seven people deep.

I was pretty sure I could cross Alyssa and Grandma off the list. And myself.

So how did I go about finding who was listed in that will? A quick online search confirmed that I could go to the courthouse and request to see it once it went into probate. Given that the lawyer who called me was probably the executor of the estate, I imagined it had already been filed with probate.

Shoving my laptop across the kitchen table, I rubbed my arms. All of this research made me want caffeine.

Coffee. My spirit animal.

. . .

BECAUSE I WAS FREEZING from the harsh reality of January weather, and because Grandma assured me she could be alone for a few hours without being in danger of setting the house on fire or locking herself out in the snow (which she thought was way more funny than I did), I drove three blocks to my neighborhood coffee shop. I could have walked, but that would be insane or for people who love winter. So, in other words, people who are not me.

I wanted a cup of hot coffee and I wanted an environment that wasn't my house to attempt to read the book Alyssa had given me. Ryan was right—this was serious business and I needed to stop bumbling along and at least attempt to improve my skills in communicating with the dead. Because currently it was mostly me being annoyed when ghosts didn't respect my boundaries. I felt like a haggard mother with three toddlers. Nothing was going to change about the situation so maybe I needed to change myself.

After ordering a latte the size of my head, I find a two-seater table in the corner, with my back to a pony wall. Ever since I was kidnapped and hit by a car, I'm a little funny about having my back exposed to the room. I surveyed the crowd, which was thin for a Thursday. But it was only four, so maybe that was why. Post-lunch crowd, too early for the after-dinner people. I'm not sure what is so appealing about sitting in a room full of wood and the scent of coffee beans with strangers, but I find it very comforting.

More daydreamer than academic, I don't read as often as I could. I tend to wander off in my thoughts mid-sentence. My sister was a huge reader as a kid but I was more into controlling my environment. You can't control a story in a book and that always seemed risky to me. But nonfiction was different. I should be able to handle facts.

Except this wasn't a book of facts. It was a guru-style spiritual book written by someone who claimed to have answers but couldn't possibly have answers, given we weren't dealing with science or stats. I was on page two still when the barista yelled, "Bailey!"

It felt like I'd been reading for an hour, not five minutes. I stood up, leaving the book on the table to claim my spot, along with my puffy coat and fuzzy hat. I took my purse with me because my mother had trained me well on the ill-intent of the human species, not to mention I was still smarting from the massive bill replacing my cell phone that was lost, aka stolen, at the funeral.

The barista was in his early twenties and was the very definition of bean-pole. He was there frequently when I came in, and friendly to me. Today he'd put a flower in the foam of my latte.

"You look cold," he said. "Think about spring."

"Thanks, it's beautiful." It made me smile.

That smile fell right off my face though when I turned around and spotted the tight sweater guy Alyssa and I had seen the week before. My shoulders stiffened and I paused with my cup raised midway to my lips.

This was a different coffee shop in a different neighborhood. What were the odds that this guy would be at this exact location when I was there?

Marner always told me he didn't believe in coincidences. I wanted to, because that was easier and safer. But I couldn't quite get myself to accept that this had happened twice, given that he was someone I had seen at Vera's funeral as well.

Seemed more than a little sketchy.

He hadn't spotted me so I dropped my gaze quickly. He was standing at the community bulletin board seeing a flyer and I fast-walked past him to my table. Was it my paranoid imagination or did it look like my book was shifted a little? I could have sworn I had left it tilted a little to the left and now it was sitting straight in front of the chair.

My heart was racing but I knew I had to play it cool. I sipped my coffee too fast and burned my tongue. Wincing I forced myself to open the book and read. I read the same page three times without comprehending a single word. Finally, when it seemed enough time had passed, I ventured a furtive glance around the room.

Tight Sweater Guy seemed to be gone.

I swiveled all the way around boldly and still no creepy guy. Well, actually, he wasn't creepy it just was creepy he popped up everywhere I was. But he wasn't there anymore. I wasn't sure if I was relieved or further creeped out. Was he a ghost? Had I lost my ability (wait, what ability?) to decipher who and what I was seeing?

Back to the book. I needed help, clearly.

Now that I was focused, something jumped out at me right away. That the role of the medium is two-fold: to be comfort and reassurance to the living that there is an afterlife, and to help the deceased move on if they want to. I mean, that's a pretty big deal in terms of both. Because if people have reassurance their loved ones are okay, wouldn't they have an easier time in life? Live a more peaceful existence? It seemed highly likely and that was a powerful gift.

I've never thought I had any particular gifts other than accessorizing. I was an okay Irish dancer, an okay student, an okay singer. But nothing that made me stand out or that people heard/saw/felt with awe.

It was kind of cool to think that maybe I had a talent. That maybe I could hone my skill to a glossy shine. And bonus. It wasn't a selfish talent. It would help others, so score.

I skimmed a few more chapters and learned about opening myself up and meditation. My coffee got cold, so I slapped the book shut and put my coat on.

Distracted, I wasn't really paying attention to my surroundings when I left the coffee shop and stepped onto a side street toward my car. Amateur mistake. But I had shoved my hands in my pockets out of instinct against the cold, and felt my phone in the pocket. Wait a minute. I had put my phone in my purse, I was sure of it. I pulled it out of the pocket and it wasn't my new could-have-taken-a-cruise-for-this-price phone. It was the one that had disappeared at the funeral.

That realization made me whip my head up and around.

Just in time to catch a fist in my face.

It was so painful and shocking I didn't even have time to react. I just crumpled to the ground, and made a half-hearted attempt to cover my face, some deep-seated survival instinct telling me if they had hit me once, they would hit me twice.

The ground was hard and cold and all I could see was stars dancing in front of my eyes.

Then I heard yelling and footsteps pounding. Scared, I tried to sit away, realizing whatever the hell was happening I needed to attempt to get back inside the coffee shop.

"Bailey, are you okay? Oh my God, that was just... crazy."

My vision had cleared and I saw it was the barista squatting in front of me, staring at me with concern. There was a woman a few feet away on the phone, saying I had been mugged. I guess she was calling 911.

Still stunned, I tentatively touched my nose. "Ow."

"I can't believe that guy hit you," the barista said, sounding outraged.

"How did you know I was in trouble?" I asked, stable in a sitting position, my ass starting to get really cold on the wet snow-covered sidewalk.

"I didn't." He held my fuzzy hat up. "You forgot your hat."

"Thank God," I said, giving a shaky laugh. The found cell phone was still in my hand. My purse was laying on the ground next to me. "I don't think they stole anything."

"That's good." He tried to put my hat on my head, but he was being appropriately cautious and my curls don't accommodate cautious. The hat just rose to the crown of my head, a cherry on the whipped cream of my curls.

I reached up and yanked it ruthlessly down to my ears, grateful for the warmth. "Can you help me up?" I said, studying his chest to see if he wore a name tag. I felt guilty for not knowing his name. No tag.

"I think you should wait until someone gets here."

"I'm sitting in snow," I said, even though that was obvious.

A cop car came around the corner and stopped in the middle of the street, lights flashing without sound.

My heart sank when I saw the driver get out. Damn it. I knew him. He was around my age and he golfed sometimes with Jake. Officer Brian Martin.

His seemed as equally displeased to see me given the way he swore without compunction. "You okay?" he asked me.

I nodded.

"Call Detective Marner," he told the other cop.

"Why?" the guy asked, clearly questioning why call homicide in when I was sitting there quite alive, thanks.

"This is his girlfriend," Brian said.

"Can we not call Marner?" I said, finding my voice. "I'm fine."

"You've got blood all over your face. I have to call him or he'll kick my ass."

"I do?" I touched my nose. My hand touched dampness. I pulled it back and saw blood. A lot of blood.

My eyes rolled back in my head and I went down with zero warning.

NINE

"WELL, THIS IS FAMILIAR," Jake said, after he'd pushed his way into the ER room I was in, flashing his badge for admittance. The worry on his face eased the second he saw me sitting up, intact. "How do you manage to find trouble everywhere you go?"

That annoyed me but I wasn't going to argue about it. "I'm just lucky that way."

Except it came out all muffled because there was dressing jammed up my nose. I had a wicked headache and I just wanted to close my eyes at home. My grandmother was blowing up my phone, worried about me, and I was worried about her. Plus I was worried that I had been targeted, not by a pickpocket, but by Tight Sweater Guy. Lots of worrying all the way around.

Jake frowned. "Did you break your nose?" He came forward and eyed my nose warily.

"I didn't break my nose," I said, more a little testily. "Some jerk who punched me in the face broke my nose."

"He *punched* you?" Jake asked, his fist clenching. "Who punched you?"

Now it was my turn to frown. I touched the sides of my nose gingerly. The doctor had given me some kind of numbing gel before he had started messing around in my nose, but it still hurt like hell. "Yes. I got mugged. What did they tell you happened?"

"That you had an accident but you were fine. I thought they meant a fender bender." He put his hand up like he wanted to touch me but then dropped it again. "What happened? Who do I need to arrest?"

"I don't know. I was looking down at my phone because the weirdest thing happened. I was in the coffee shop and there was this guy there that I saw at Vera's funeral and last week at a different coffee shop. I swear. Alyssa can verify this." I paused for breath.

I wasn't sure he was even listening to me. He was stroking my arm, staring at my nose, and looking very upset.

"Does my nose look that bad?" I asked, starting to get concerned.

"It looks... painful. You already have bruising under your eyes." His thumb gently ran over the skin below my lashes. "I want to kill whoever did this."

"I doubt we'll ever figure out who did it." That was more than a little infuriating. "Which sucks, because if my nose ends up crooked, I need to know who to sue." I didn't want to end up looking like Owen Wilson. He can pull it off because he's tall, charming, and funny as hell. I couldn't pull it off.

Jake kissed my forehead. "We'll figure it out. There is probably CTC footage. Is the doctor coming back? I want to hear what he has to say."

"He's going to say my nose is broken." I wanted to ask Jake to hand me my purse so I could look at my compact mirror, but at the same time I was too scared to. My entire face felt swollen and I didn't think I could handle seeing my battered face. I don't think I'm overly vain, but I like to put my best foot forward. Or best face forward.

"Did you eat dinner?" Jake asked.

"No." I rubbed my temples. "But I just want to go home."

I felt tired, testy, and in pain, and my cranky voice made that pretty obvious.

He gingerly petted my hair. "Okay, sweetie. I'm going to go find the doctor."

"Thank you."

While Jake was gone I couldn't resist. I swung my legs over the side of the bed and went for my purse. I dug my compact mirror out and flipped it open. And immediately slapped it shut again.

Oh my word, I looked like an alien version of myself. Exaggerated and distorted. There was bruising under my eyes already but it wasn't that bad. What was hideous was my honker. I have a tiny Irish nose, which fits my fairly small face. I have thin-ish lips and a dusting of freckles. The wide nose from the swelling made my cheekbones and mouth virtually disappear.

The packing in my nose was protruding from my nostril and was smattered with blood.

I was not my best self at the moment.

Sighing, I shoved the mirror back in my purse.

Since I was Marner's girlfriend, the cops had brought me to the hospital. I could hear them talking to him outside of my room, expressing concern for me. He assured them I was fine, at which point they shifted to giving him crap about needing to keep me safer.

"She should conceal and carry," Brian said. "And I'm being serious."

"Are you out of your mind?" Jake asked. "Have you seen what she gets into? She'd shoot herself in the foot."

Well, that seemed a little insulting and exaggerated.

I'm not clumsy. I just get attacked a lot.

"I can hear you," I said, loudly. There was nothing but a curtain between us.

The curtain ripped back. My boyfriend's sheepish face appeared, his free hand tugging on his tie at the neck. "The nurse is coming in with your discharge paperwork."

I didn't even bother to answer him. I hadn't been required to put on a gown since it was obvious what the issue was, so when the nurse popped in with a smile, all that was needed was her reading the discharge instructions and having me sign them.

"Is that your boyfriend out there?" she asked in a low voice. "Very cute." She gave me a wink.

"Which guy?" I asked, and I didn't mean that testily. For all I knew, she was talking about Brian.

She laughed. "The hot one in the suit who stormed in here ready to rough up whoever hurt you."

"Oh. Yeah. That's him." That made me feel a little better. It's never a bad thing for another woman to think your boyfriend is hot. "He thinks I'm accident prone. Which maybe I am."

Or maybe I'd just been exposed to a lot of murderers lately. That ups the risk factor.

"Just don't take up roller blading. I've seen more broken bones from that than anything else."

"I don't see that happening, trust me. I'm not athletic."

"Can I come in?" Jake asked, as he was walking in.

The nurse gave him a brilliant smile. "She's all yours."

"Lucky me," Jake murmured and I couldn't tell if it was sarcasm or not.

I stood up, paperwork in hand. "I need to go get my car. It's at the coffee shop."

"I'll go get it later. You shouldn't be driving tonight." He took the paperwork out of my hand and lifted my purse up and gave it to me. "Are you hungry?"

"No." The thought of chewing with my throbbing nose and head was very unappealing. "Though I wouldn't turn down a milkshake."

That made him laugh. "You will always eat like a nine-year-old, won't you?"

Hey, I like what I like. "Not always. Just when I'm in a hurry. Or on a road trip." Or on any day when he wasn't cooking for me.

"Okay, let's get you a milkshake."

The cops had waited to see that I was okay. I knew they were all serious about finding out who hit me but I already knew who it was. Tight Sweater Guy. I just needed to put the pieces together as to who he was, given he had been at Vera's funeral.

"Hey, Rocky," Brian said to me when he saw me come toward the lobby. "Next time duck."

"Got it. Thanks for making sure I was okay."

"No problem. Glad it wasn't more serious."

When we stepped outside, the wind made my eyes water, but the cold actually felt good on my swollen nose. I kept touching it, and then catching myself doing it. I needed to leave it alone. The doctor said it would heal fine, but I was a little terrified I might look like a prize fighter who lost.

"Jake, my phone magically reappeared in my pocket," I told him, pulling it out as a visual aid. "It wasn't there before, I swear it."

He gave me a look and I knew exactly what he was thinking. That it had been there all along and I was a ditz who had been looking for it all over that funeral home when it was legitimately on my person.

"At least you have it back. Maybe you can sell it and recoup some of that money."

That was not the point. I made a noncommittal sound. "We need to get Grandma a milkshake too or she'll be furious with us. She loves dairy."

"Whatever you say, babe."

The street we were crossing was icy and I was holding my nose just in case I fell. I'm not sure what that was going to do, but I didn't want further damage. Logically, it would make better sense to have my hands free to protect my booty if I fell, but I can't say I'm always the most logical person.

So I was looking at my feet and covering a portion of my face and not really looking at my surroundings until I happened to glance up.

There he was. Tight Sweater Guy.

It was like an old movie. I swear my mental camera zoomed in on his face and we made eye contact. I was tempted to hiss, "You," to make the cliché fully complete but I'm not that cinematic. Instead I screamed and hit my boyfriend's arm. "That's the guy in the coffee shop! I think he's the guy who punched me."

Fortunately, Marner is not your average, regular-guy boyfriend who might have said, "What?" and asked for further explanation. Instead, with zero hesitation, he went straight up to the guy.

"Hey! What are you doing here?" he asked the guy. "Are you following this woman?"

"What? No. Of course not." The man had gone pale and as I got closer, and more importantly, Marner got closer, he started glancing left and right for an escape.

It was obvious he was going to bolt and it took about two seconds for Marner to get him down on the ground.

Once he had him secure, he called Officer Martin on his cell. "Need you in the parking garage to question a suspect."

"Is this who hit you?" he asked me. "Can you positively identify him?"

"I can positively say he was in the coffee shop and left right before I got attacked. But I didn't see who hit me."

This guy was obviously not used to being in a supine position on a parking garage floor. He wasn't really resisting. But he did say, "I'm calling the cops. Then I'm suing you."

"I am the cops," Marner told him. "And so are they." He gestured to Brian, and the other officer, whose name I couldn't remember.

"What's up?" Brian asked.

"Bailey said this guy was following her at the coffee shop." He hauled the guy to his feet and handed him over. "I think you should ask him some questions."

"This is insane," the guy said.

I was plagued with doubt. So the guy had been in the same place at the same time as me three times. That could happen. Just thinking that made me realize most likely, no, that could not happen. Sure, a coffee shop I frequented a lot. But the ER? An hour after the coffee shop? Highly doubtful. I would let Marner and the other cops do their job and if this guy was totally innocent then that would be that. But I strongly suspected not only was he the guy who had punched me, he was the person who had put the phone back in my pocket.

Time for a milkshake.

We went to a place that had alcohol-infused shakes and I chose the vanilla, apple pie, and bourbon one. I got a virgin version for Grandma.

As we were walking into my house, me sucking the final delicious remnant of ice cream up through the straw, Jake's phone rang. I was used to him answering calls so I just went into the living room and found Grandma watching TV.

"I got you a milkshake," I told her, handing it over. "Vanilla and apple pie."

"Thanks. That nose is something and none of it is good."

I sighed. I was going to get a lot of double takes in public the next few days. "I know. But the doctor says it will heal fine."

"I'll say a prayer."

I needed it. "Thanks."

Jake shut the front door and kicked his dress shoes off. "Do you know a guy named Devin Whittaker?"

The name meant nothing. "Nope."

"That's the guy in the garage's name. They're running background on him, but without any witnesses and you unable to point the finger at him, we've got nothing to hold him on."

I would be more outraged at the fact if I hadn't been kidnapped before, hit by a car, and held at gunpoint. A fist to the face seemed not that bad, all things considered. "Thanks for trying."

He said hello to my grandmother and asked her and me both if we needed anything.

"I'm good. They gave me ibuprofen in the hospital."

"I could use some water," Grandma said.

I had sat down next to her and I started to get up, but Jake held out his palm. "I've got it. You just take it easy."

"He's a nice boy," Grandma said as he went into the kitchen. "You really should marry him."

"He's Italian," I reminded her, hoping that would change the subject away from marriage.

"So? At least he's Catholic."

Living together, the three of us, was going to be so much fun. Not.

I WAS SITTING on the living room floor the next morning with my eyes closed when I heard the shuffling of slippers.

"What are you doing?" Grandma asked.

"I'm meditating." Trying to learn to control my thoughts as they pertained to the spirit world, per my handy-dandy guide to spiritual mediumship.

"I guess that's better than doing drugs."

"I one hundred percent agree with you." Though so far I wasn't sold on this concept. Nothing much of anything seemed to be happening. "I'm supposed to devote several hours once a week to letting the dead come to me, and the rest of the week ban them so all our needs are met."

"I don't see any ghosts."

"Me either." I squeezed my eyes tighter as I concentrated, which only made spots dance behind my lids. Nothing. Not even Ryan. Where had he been? If we had this quota shouldn't he be around more?

When I opened my eyes, my grandmother was standing in front of me wearing a retro track suit. Sweatband and all. It was a glorious shade of burgundy with pink stripes down the pant legs. "Are you an extra in an eighties movie?" I asked her. I mean, it was possible. Films are frequently being made in Cleveland because it's cheaper than New York.

"What? No. I have Jazzercise."

That confused me, as did the sweatband. Was she really going to work up actual perspiration? "Where?"

"The rec center. I go every Thursday."

"Oh, okay. Let me make sure I close this portal or whatever that I attempted to open then we can go." She was working out more than I was, so I really couldn't deny her that right.

"Gotcha. If you see Vera tell her thanks for the cheddar. I appreciate her thinking of me."

"Of course." I realized I hadn't asked Grandma what she planned to do with her five grand, but that could wait for the car ride. I had a portal to close and all. I grabbed the book and scanned the chapter again but it wasn't particularly clear to me how to tell the dead to back off once I was doing being "open."

"See you all next Thursday," I said. "Until then, respect my privacy." That seemed good enough. Polite. But decisive.

"I'm ready," I said, standing up. "I'll get our coats."

"I think you're getting good at this medium stuff," Grandma said. "You sound very authoritative."

"You think so? Thanks. I'm definitely getting the hang of it."

Yeah. No, I wasn't.

Bingo proved that. Big-time.

TEN

I HAD zero intention of playing bingo because the regulars are too intense.

My plan was to talk to all the ladies who knew Vera and see what was what with the big brouhaha.

But the dead had a different plan in mind.

On Thursday no one had wanted to acknowledge my "come on in for a limited time" offer to talk.

Yet Friday night shenanigans were clearly universal even when you were dead. They were out full force and ready to party.

"Who beat you up?" Grandma's friend Shirley asked when we went into the basement at church.

"I got punched walking to my car but I didn't see who it was," I told her. There was no sugarcoating it with these women. They wanted proof that crime was rampant and society was crumbling.

"You can't go anywhere alone anymore," she said, shaking her head. "It's a gosh darn shame."

Marianne, who was still dying her hair the color of a Twinkie, pushed her glasses up on her nose. "Oh, dear. Bailey Margaret, your poor little button nose. It will never be the same."

My worst fear verbalized by Marianne. "The doctor seems to think it will be okay."

Marianne made a sound that indicated she didn't believe it would ever be the same.

Shirley made a similar clucking sound.

I touched my nose self-consciously. My under-eyes were still bruised and my nose still swollen. I hadn't thought it would be that bad to show my face at bingo but now I wasn't so sure.

"You look fine," Grandma told me. "Stop touching your nose."

I dropped my hand. I got Grandma settled at the table with her friends and started running errands for them all, getting cards and soft drinks and nachos for Shirley. I was stunned at the sheer volume of processed food available at the snack bar, manned by middle school kids and their parents. The kids were mostly screwing around, the parents mostly frantic, yelling for a popcorn or a Skittles with the importance of an air traffic controller.

The kid who handed me the nachos basically threw them at me, the jalapenos Shirley had requested flying off the tortilla chip pile with a spin of the little plastic container. I stopped them from rolling off the counter and onto the floor and scooped everything up into my hands. I turned around and almost collided with a priest with slicked-back hair. "Oh! Sorry, Father."

"You can see me?" he asked, and made a move like he was going to grab my shoulders.

Oh, no. "Um..." I glanced around, trying to gauge what the reaction of other people around us were. There was an Asian woman smiling at me. Nothing else.

"You've got a handful," she said.

I smiled back at her. "Bingo brings on the munchies, apparently."

She looked to be in her early thirties and she nodded. "I've got my grandparents with me and they have in a request for Dippin' Dots. I feel like that is something to look forward to with age. You revert to the treats of childhood as your snacks."

"That is something to look forward to," I said, most sincerely. "Have fun."

I walked away. The priest was following me. His form shifted as he got way too close to me. I realized that the cut of his pants and shirt, along with his enormous glasses, put him as having probably died in the eighties or early nineties. Being trapped at bingo for thirty years seemed like the very definition of purgatory to me.

"Did you see the man?" the priest asked me, way too close to my ear for comfort.

I shook my head to indicate no as I started setting snacks down on the table Grandma and her friends were at.

He sounded manic. Very frantic. "He's after me. The man who steals from the collection. I caught him."

This guy was creeping me out. I could feel his cold presence. It seemed to tease against my back, pressing through the thick wool of my sweater and tickle across my hair. This was the first time I felt like I could actually sense a spirit's fear. It seemed like fear and isolation had driven him to a state of repetitive incoherency.

"Did you see the man?" he asked. "He's after me. Did you see the man?"

I closed my eyes and tried to remember what I was supposed to say to banish spirits who were unwanted. I chanted in my head that he needed to respect my boundaries, that I couldn't help him right now.

"Why are your eyes closed?" a high-pitched voice asked me. "Are you high?"

I opened my eyes and turned to Shirley, who was eyeing me with suspicion. "I'm not high, I promise."

"You know there's a drug crisis going on right now."

"I know, but I can assure you I don't have any issues that way." I had a lot of other issues but that wasn't one of them. "I just got dizzy for a second."

"Low blood sugar," Shirley said with confidence. "Eat a Skittles."

"I think she drinks too much caffeine," Grandma said.

That was entirely possible. I had leaned forward onto the table wanting away from the priest so I couldn't feel his presence. I darted a quick glance over my shoulder to see if he was gone. I jumped slightly. He was gone but Vera was standing there.

"I miss these girls even if they are backstabbing biddies," she said. "And that Shirley is a tightwad. She'll never pay you for those nachos, just so you know."

I nodded, though I had never expected her to pay for them. It was meant to be a nice gesture on my part. "So what do you all think happened to Vera?" I asked the table of five women, cutting right to the chase. Bingo was due to start in ten minutes and once the balls rolled and numbers called, there was no talking.

"This should be interesting," Vera said. "I wish I had a drink for this."

"What do I think happened to her?" Patricia asked. "I think she got drunk and fell in the snow. She was always a bit of a booze bag."

"A booze bag?" Vera asked, indignantly. "I have always been a woman who could handle her liquor. Just because Patricia is a teetotaler doesn't make me a booze bag."

"But why would she go outside?" I asked. "That just really puzzles me."

"Maybe she thought she saw a man," Marianne said, and they all snickered.

"I think she mixed up her pill days and got loopy," Grandma said. "That's easy enough to do. She probably thought she was going into the laundry room when she was actually going outside."

"Who the hell does that?" Vera asked. "Even high on pain pills I'm not blind."

"What does anyone know about her neighbor? Do you think they could have pushed her outside and stolen her pills? There is a drug crisis going on right now. Shirley's right."

Shirley paused with a nacho midway to her mouth. "Well, that sounds shady. Were pills missing?"

"They were scattered all over."

"People on drugs will do anything," Marianne said, nodding

her head. "It's possible. Us elderly ladies living alone are such obvious targets, it's terrifying. That's why I have a security system."

"But if he was her neighbor, she probably just let him in," Grandma said.

"None of them know anything," Vera said, waving her hand.

"He's after me," the priest said, reappearing behind Shirley on the opposite side of the table.

An elderly woman was shuffling past and she stopped and stared at me. "Who are you?" she asked. "Why don't you help me?"

Oh, boy. Another ghost. I guess it made sense that in a church basement there would be quite the collection of the dead. Lots of funerals upstairs.

"It's just a shame," I said, generically, hoping that covered everyone in my presence.

"Vera lived a good life," Patricia said. "I don't see the shame in that."

"Besides, she was a class act, leaving us money," Marianne added.

"Damn right I'm classy," Vera said.

The friendly woman I had spoken to earlier smiled at me and slid into the seat next to Shirley. "This is the first time I've ever met someone like you," she said. "My grandparents and I have been here... I'm not sure how long. But a long time."

The cute lady with the bob and the sweet smile was dead? That was a bummer. "I'll get back to you on that," I told her, making direct eye contact so she would know I was talking to her.

"You'll get back to me on whether I'm classy or not?" Vera asked. "I see," she added, sounding miffed.

"What's that supposed to mean?" Shirley asked. "Are you saying it wasn't right for Vera to leave us money?"

"Of course she isn't," Grandma said. "She got money from Vera too!"

"I don't understand," the Asian woman said.

"He's after me," the priest said.

"You need to help me," the old lady said.

There were way too many people talking. My head felt like it was on a swivel and all their comments were jumbling together.

I was contemplating claiming I had urgent diarrhea and running out of the room when they called the start of bingo.

"Shh!" Patricia said, even though no one living was actually speaking.

"U sixty-nine," a man's voice came from behind me. I didn't even need to turn around to know that was Ryan. I knew his voice and his infantile sense of humor.

I swiped one of Grandma's Skittles and chewed it so I didn't say anything out loud that would make me sound insane.

But when the priest said, "He's after me," again and Vera started running commentary on Marianne's orange lipstick, I couldn't stop myself.

"My office hours are on Thursdays," I said. "Three to six p.m."

While the bingo ladies all looked at me like I was bananas, the Asian woman nodded. "Thank you," she said.

Hopefully she could tell time and what day of the week it was. Otherwise she might appear at four in the morning while I was sleeping. I was also assuming that she could find me, but I suspected it was more like she could follow me now that she had made contact with me.

My house was getting more crowded by the minute.

Patricia was stamping away on her ten cards with a vigor that belied her age. "Bailey Margaret, can you get me a cup of coffee?"

"Sure." I stood up and gave a small gesture to Vera to follow me. "What do you think?" I murmured under my breath.

"About what?"

"Any suspects?" I looked like a mad mutterer but I didn't care.

"From these girls?" Vera shook her head. "Not a chance. None of them knew they were getting any money from me. Plus, none of them drive solo anymore."

Good point. "Excellent. My list is getting smaller."

Until the next day when I went to the courthouse and pulled

Vera's will. There it was. A list of fifty names. I took a picture with my phone and sighed.

I could cross off the bingo ladies, myself, Alyssa, and Grandma. That left forty-three names. I didn't even bother to look at them. I didn't want to get overwhelmed.

Researching that was going to have to wait until Monday. I had a date with Jake to assemble Grandma's new bedroom furniture.

Because that's what our Saturday night fun was now.

Woo hoo.

"HELLO, IS THIS RICHARD ROBERTSON?" I asked, using my best important-person voice.

"Yes, who is this?"

"This is Bailey Burke, a friend of Vera Rosenbaum."

"Oh, dear, yes. Poor Vera. It's hard to believe she's gone. I wish I could have seen her one last time." His voice was gravelly and a little shaky.

"From what everyone has told me, she meant a lot to you and vice versa."

"She was my soulmate. The only girl for me."

I wasn't going to mention I didn't think the same held true for Vera. "It seems like a very passionate relationship."

He gave a rusty laugh. "That's a great way to put it. So, you're a friend, you say? What can I do for you, young lady?"

I paced the kitchen, hoping Grandma couldn't hear me from the other room. "I was talking to Stanley about you and Vera still being close and I was just wondering if you knew the contents of her will before she died. Her niece and nephew are quite upset."

"Gold diggers," he said emphatically. "Both of them. What do they know about sacrifice? Do you know how Vera got her money?"

I had assumed through her marriages but mostly her family. "Her parents, from what I understand."

"Exactly. Her father got out of Germany way ahead of Hitler's rise to power. He saw the writing on the wall and left money and power and property behind to start all over in New York in the diamond district. He worked his behind off and made a fortune. What do those two knuckleheads know about sacrifice or hard work? Vera's sister gave them everything and they still want more."

Interesting. I had suspected the "knuckleheads" were greedy, but here was an outside opinion verifying that. Richard had nothing to gain or lose from being honest. "That's a shame. Your son doesn't seem that way at all." Stanley was definitely pretentious but he seemed like he had his own success and money.

"Who, Stanley? Money definitely isn't what motivates him."

I couldn't read the tone of his voice.

"Have you spoken to Stanley recently? I haven't been able to get in touch with him." I hadn't tried, but that was beside the point. "When did he get back to LA?"

"No reason to be worried. I've heard from him every day. He's a good kid that way. We didn't use to be close but I've tried to repair our relationship the last few years."

"So you've seen him?" This wasn't really getting me anywhere. I didn't know how to ask the right leading questions. I needed to take a class on interrogation. Right after I learned how to be a medium.

"No, he's still in Cleveland. He said he wanted to stay to help settle Vera's affairs."

That was interesting. "Oh, how nice of him. Is he still at the Ritz?"

"I believe so, yes. He does love the Ritz."

That seemed in direct contradiction to him saying Stanley wasn't motivated by money. Personally, in three meetings it had seemed to me Stanley liked the finer things. But I guess there is a difference between enjoying material possessions and being motivated by them.

"Thank you for talking to me. I appreciate it. I'll give Stanley another call."

"Do you know what my favorite memory of Vera is?" Richard asked, out of the blue.

The Oscars in '63? I coughed into my hand. "I'm sure you have quite a few."

"Oh, I do, but my favorite memory of her is one night we had gone to Whiskey-a-Go-Go. That was all the rage then and we were much older than a lot of the other partiers. Vera laughed about it, said that these girls were wasting their youth on doing blow mostly nude."

There had to be more to this story because this did not sound particularly romantic. "Uh-huh."

"So we left because honestly I only had eyes for Vera and it was getting comical. We drove up into the Hills and hiked through the canyon about fifty yards, carrying a bottle of gin. We sat down and stared down at Los Angeles and I told her that I want every moment to be that like, because it was perfect. We felt alive, and in love. And she told me, for her, every moment was like that. That she disdained the mundane and embraced each moment in and of itself as excitement and perfection. That's beautiful, don't you think?"

I mean, it was. But I'm a practical girl raised in a practical town by practical parents and grandparents. It all seemed well and good to feel that way when you were born with a silver spoon in your mouth. But it's hard to imagine steel workers thought every moment was exciting. Or the women who had to empty trash bins inside motel rooms.

For most people, I figured life was pretty even with notable highs and lows.

"That is beautiful," I said, because what else could I say? *Bully for Vera?*

I did think there was merit is appreciating life, the time you have, the people you get to spend it with. For sure. So in that regard, I was being truthful.

Richard was just getting warmed up. It seemed he either was lonely or everyone in his life was tired of indulging his favorite subjects of Vera and boozing back in the sixties and seventies. He talked about pool parties, all-nighters at Frank Sinatra's place in

Palm Springs, getting smashed at the red-carpet premiere of Mary Poppins (I mean, what? Who did that?), and doing the dirty with Vera under a stairwell in a hallway at the Chateau Martmont, pre-surveillance cameras.

If that's what it took to "feel alive" I was okay feeling half-dead because yuck. Under-the-stairwell sex was not my thing and I didn't think Jake would ever want that either.

At some point, Richard seemed to realize he'd strayed into "indelicate territory" as he called it and apologized. "I'm sorry, young lady. I'm not at a poker game. Forgive an old man for indulging in days when I could move without creaking. Nowadays my only excitement is when they serve cheesecake at lunch."

"Cheesecake is pretty exciting," I said. "I have a sweet tooth. And I don't mind. I appreciate your stories. That's why I enjoyed spending time with Vera and my grandmother."

After we hung up the phone I sat there, biting my lip and pondering a world where there were no cell phones and people didn't frown on smoking. Probably a good thing I hadn't been alive then. I would have been a chain smoker, let's be honest. As it was, I fought the urge to reach for nicotine whenever I was stressed, though I had to give myself props for not vaping in recent weeks with all the chaos of Mom's heart attack and Vera's death.

Since I had actually texted Stanley twice and gotten short responses that had indicated to me he was no longer interested in being friendly, I didn't bother to text him. I just wanted to confirm he was at the Ritz.

Lo and behold, he was not. In fact, he'd never been there. They had no clue who Stanley Robertson was. Maybe they just weren't allowed to tell me, but my gut told me they were being forthcoming. Stanley had never been there. I would have chalked it up to his father being confused except that I was positive Stanley had told me that's where he was staying. Unless he meant that theoretically. Like "life is hard at the Ritz" but not that he was literally at the Ritz.

That seemed like a stretch. Most likely, he was pretending to be wealthier than he was. Or more impressive, anyway.

No one thought my life was impressive. That was one advantage to having perpetually frizzy hair and a propensity to get injured.

"Hey, Grandma," I said, heading into the living room. "How does a spa day sound? Here at home, I mean. I have one of those foot baths you can use while I paint my nails."

"Can we order pizza?"

"Absolutely."

My life may not be the Ritz Carlton, but I thought it was a pretty awesome way to spend a Sunday afternoon.

ELEVEN

I STUCK to my plan to look at Vera's will on Monday and start picking through the names. I was sitting upstairs at home in my office with my fuzzy slippers on. I had on yoga pants and a sweater that covered me from ear to knee. No sign of temperatures increasing at all and the thermostat outside was hovering around six degrees, actual temperature. None of this wind chill stuff to make it sound worse. Just legit, straight-up it's absolutely-freezing-cold six degrees.

Sipping tea in an attempt to be healthy (antioxidants, right?) I entered the first five names into my computer one by one, trying to find something that would indicate they had the potential to be a killer. Which seemed futile. Did sneaky killers make it obvious online they were killers? Doubtful, hence the descriptor "sneaky." Nothing suspicious was jumping out at me until I got to the sixth name on the list.

Devin Whittaker.

Why did that name sound so familiar?

I tapped my pen I'd been using to make notes next to names on my lower lip. Devin Whittaker.

Then it hit me and I sat straight up.

Tight Sweater Guy. I was almost positive.

I called Jake, who was at work.

"Hey, what's up?" he said.

"Can you talk for a minute?"

"Yep. Just looking at autopsy photos on a suspected gang shooting."

Yuck. I'm not good with blood. Thus explaining why I was the world's worst evidence tech at the police department during my short tenure. "Does it look like an easy case?" I asked.

"Maybe. No one's talking but there are surveillance cameras at the intersection. Just waiting for access to them."

"That's good."

"What's up, baby? Are you calling to say you love me?"

We never did that so the very thought of it made me smile. "Someday I just might, you never know. But that day is not today. I'm actually calling because I pulled Vera's will to see who else is inheriting five grand and guess whose name is on it?" I felt excited just thinking about it.

Marner sighed. "I don't know. Me?"

"What? No. Why would Vera give you money? Devin Whittaker, the guy who was in the parking garage at Metro. Isn't that crazy?"

There was a pause. "So why is he following you?"

"I don't know. It just proves that I'm not nuts and that he was at Vera's funeral, like I said all along." I hadn't actually thought through the implications of any of it.

"That's weird."

"What's weird?"

"This guy."

"So what do we do?"

"You don't do anything. You stay at home with the doors locked."

I wrinkled my nose. "Do you think I'm in danger?"

"Bailey. Someone broke your nose. Possibly him. Yes, I think you could be in danger."

I glanced over at the mirror hanging on my wall. My nose still didn't look right. It was a little swollen and just a tinge crooked. "Do you think I'm ugly? I don't think my nose is healing right."

"Oh my God. How did you go from me being worried about your safety to thinking your nose is ugly?"

"Because I don't think it's healing as fast as it should. It looks crooked." I made a face at myself in the mirror, completely losing focus on the matter at hand.

"It looks like a nose that was just broken. It will be totally normal in a month."

"Are you sure?"

"One hundred percent. Now can we talk about this guy who seems to be following you?"

Right. That guy. "Maybe it's a coincidence. Maybe he just lives in the neighborhood." Though that seemed far-fetched. But I didn't really want to think he was following me because, if he was, he had to be the killer. Or connected to the killer.

"It's possible, but I don't like it. If he's going to follow you, I'm going to follow him. Let's see how he likes a tail on his ass."

That would work. "That's a good idea."

His voice lowered. "I have a lot of good ideas."

"Most of them involving what to cook for dinner," I said cheerfully. "Speaking of, what are we having tonight?"

"I know what *I'm* having."

"That's not on the menu. Grandma will be around, remember?"

He groaned. "Is it April yet? At least when we're living together we have the excuse of going to bed every night."

"It's the middle of January. The cold, dark, domain of Old Man Winter. April is a dream that I can't even contemplate right now or I'll lose my mind entirely."

"Okay, then. Guess no sex for me." There was a shuffling sound, like he had his phone on his shoulder. "Hey, by the way, my vacation request was approved. We can book our flights to Florida soon."

"That's the sweetest thing you've ever said to me."

We ended the call and I went back to staring at Devin Whittaker's name. Then I did an online search to see what I could find. He didn't appear to have any social media presence which seemed odd for a forty-year-old. All I could manage to find was his name in an article about a local theater. He had been in Fiddler on the Roof. Maybe that's how Vera knew him. She was big into theater, and supporting the arts in general.

When I was about to give up, I found an address for him in Lakewood. It was a high-rise building on the lake and it was actually listed for sale. I called the agent. "Yes, I would love to see the condo you have listed at Winton Place. My mother is in the market."

"I'd be happy to show you the unit. It's fully remodeled."

I could see that as I scrolled through the images online. "Are you available Monday evening?"

"How does seven sound?"

"Perfect." I hoped Mom didn't have any other plans, because she was my cover. I could pretend to be shopping for a condo on my own, but my mother was much more believable because she actually was looking to buy.

It didn't look like Devin Whittaker had moved out of his condo. There were clothes in the shot of the master closet.

What I was expecting to find, I had no idea, but what I was learning about investigation was you had to turn over every stone. It was a lot of drudgery filled with dead ends.

I called my mother. "I found a condo I think you'd like to see. Are you free on Monday?"

"If I'm going to see one, I might as well see a bunch. Let my call my agent and stack a dozen or so."

I tensed immediately. A dozen? That was going to challenge my patience and optimism.

But what choice did I have, really?

"Sounds good. This one is at seven, so maybe we can start around four?"

"Let's start at three. I don't want to be rushed."

I did. "Great!"

Hopefully there would be time in there for dinner because I was going to need a glass of wine.

THE GHOSTS WERE DRIVING me absolutely nuts. Everywhere I turned I saw someone new. At the bar, at my parents' house, in my own living room. Most of them didn't speak and they didn't stick around. Or if they did speak, it was like the priest—stuck on repeat.

"I totally jacked this up," I told Alyssa. "I should have read the whole book you gave me before I started meditating and telling dead people what to do. These people are everywhere. And no one showed up for the office hours I instituted. That was basically the only time things were quiet. It's like somehow I reversed it."

We were spending Saturday morning at the West Side Market, a huge venue of local food stalls. Alyssa had it in her head she was going to start cooking and she was currently standing in front of a fish stall checking out stone crabs. "You jumped into it like I would, not like you normally do. You're usually the study-and-plan-ahead, girl."

"I wanted results," I said, shrugging, and unwrapping my thick scarf from around my neck. It was hot in the market with heaters blowing and bodies crammed in. The market has a unique smell of meat and pasties and floor cleaners. The earthy scent of fresh produce ushered you into the building, then it gave way to the acrid odor of raw seafood and beef.

As a kid, my father had acted like it was a treat for me to go to the market with him. Sure, the crepes were delicious and time with him was always something I had craved, but rows and rows of animal eyeballs staring back at you on ice was not the stuff of seven-year-olds' dreams.

Now I could appreciate the sheer variety and enjoy buying some of the ready-made food, but I was no foodie and I hated to cook, so I was more there with Alyssa for moral support.

"What do you think, Chilean sea bass?" she asked.

"Are you sure you want to start with seafood?" I asked, looking suspiciously at the variety of fish lying there.

"Um, yes, because I can't give myself food poisoning if I undercook it. I could kill myself if I try chicken."

Yikes. "Good point. This is why I let Jake do all the cooking."

"Yeah, well, I don't have a cute cop boyfriend who likes to braise things. I have to fend for myself and you have to start somewhere with meat." She raised her eyebrows when the fish guy coughed. "That was truly an accident, not an innuendo," she said. "I swear."

He looked amused. "I bet. For the record, I can braise things. And I know when meat is done."

"Oh, really?" Interest creeped into her voice and she looked him up and down.

I sipped my coffee and waited until this played out. Men flirted with Alyssa everywhere we went. This guy was muscular, arms covered in tattoos, chin hidden behind a full beard. "Really. You have to touch meat to know when it's done. You can't just eyeball it."

Alyssa gave him a look that said *I know where this is going, son.* But she didn't totally shut him down. "So what do you suggest I buy?"

"King crab legs. We'll boil them together." He gave her a confident grin.

But Alyssa wasn't usually an easy sell. "I'll take the sea bass," she said dryly. "Whatever you think is an appropriate portion for one woman who likes to eat like a normal person, not a supermodel. And write your number or Snapchat on it."

She rolled her eyes at me but I could tell she thought he was cute.

He hustled to get her fish and wrapped it. With a marker he wrote his number and his name on it. After she paid and they enjoyed a few more flirty words we walked away and turned the corner. "Damn it," she said, glancing at her fish wrapper. "His name is Sebastian. That is so not fair."

"Why?" I spied French macarons and got excited. "What's wrong with the name Sebastian?"

"Nothing. It's both somehow adorable and sexy all at once. It's nerdy yet rocker. It's cruel to be introduced to a man with a name like that because it's highly doubtful I can resist going out with him. Why would his mother do that to me?"

"I strongly suspect that's not what his parents were plotting when they named him."

"You never know. Now what vegetable goes with Sebastian's sea bass?"

"You're asking the wrong person. Ask Google." I found myself drawn to the macarons like a strong sugar current. "I need to buy these."

"Get a salted caramel one for me. I'm going in pursuit of greens."

"Meet me back here."

She gave me a wave and pressed through the throng of shoppers. I was staring at the mesmerizing rows of colorful little treats when I felt the warm inside air shift with a cool breeze. Not thinking anything of it I just instinctively glanced to my right. Then standing up straight, heart racing.

It was the woman from bingo, who had been so friendly to me when I was buying snacks. The one who was dead.

It occurred to me I didn't even know if her grandparents were dead or not. I had just assumed they were since she'd said they were with her. But were they really or was that just what was going down when she had died?

"Hi," she said, with another friendly smile. "I'm so glad you're here."

"Can I help you?" I asked, holding my phone up to my ear in my usual don't-look-like-a-psycho move.

"I've never met someone like you," she said, again smiling. "I'm just so happy to see you."

She was older than I had thought originally, probably in her mid-thirties. "I'm very new to this," I told her. "My skill set isn't amazing."

"I just need someone to find my body."

Oh, here we go. The body hunt. The last time I'd gone off in search of a body I had gotten myself in all kinds of scrapes. "Do you know where it is?" That might be wishful thinking but it was a good starting point.

To my shock, she nodded. "It's in my backyard. My ex-husband killed me and buried me in the yard, then poured a patio over top."

I gasped. "What a bastard."

"I know, right? I should have listened to my parents and married a man like my father. He told everyone I cheated on him and that's why we split, and that I left with another man. I would never, ever have left my son. He was only three years old at the time."

"Oh, geez, I'm so sorry. What's your address?"

A big guy carrying a toddler walked straight through the woman. The little boy started wailing instantly.

Poor kid. He instinctively knew a ghost was present. I wondered how old her son would be now but it seemed rude to ask when she had died.

She gave me her address and I pulled my phone down so I could type it into my notes. It was in Fairview Park, an area of primarily bungalows. I wondered how anyone could bury a body with no one noticing. "And I'm sorry, what's your name?"

"It's Margaret Henley."

I felt an affinity for her. "My middle name is Margaret."

"I know, I heard the women at bingo saying your name." She gave me another sincere smile. "Thank you. You don't know what this means to me. I don't want my son to think that his mother left him."

I nodded, a lump in my throat. "And your ex's name?"

"Michael."

I realized there was a woman staring at me behind Margaret. I had forgotten my ruse of talking on the phone once I had started taking notes. Whoops. "I'll get back to you," I said.

Then, heart thumping, though I wasn't exactly sure why, I turned back to the case of macarons. "Can I get a dozen?" I said when the girl behind the counter asked if she could help me. They were small and Grandma had a sweet tooth.

By the time I was done selecting my flavors, Alyssa was back and Margaret was gone.

"I choked and got asparagus," she said, holding up a bag.

"I think that goes totally fine with sea bass."

"I wanted to get crazy and experiment but I guess next time. What kind of wine?"

"White goes with fish."

"Great. If you're done we can head out and hit the store for some wine."

"I'm done." I took my bag from the clerk and handed her my debit card. "Hey, do you think if I tell the cops that I think there might be a body buried in the backyard of a person who I have no connection to whatsoever, they'll take me serious?"

Alyssa paused in the process of pointing out which macaron she wanted to the clerk. "No. They'll think you're a nutjob."

"That's what I thought." I was going to have to see if anyone had ever even filed a missing persons report on Margaret. Damn it. I should have asked her for a date. This was going to be harder without that information.

"Did you just see a ghost?"

"Yep. She said her ex buried her in the backyard."

"What a dick."

"I think that would be accurate." The market was crowded in this corner and the cashier young and female. She wasn't listening to us at all.

She handed me my card back with a smile and turned to Alyssa. "Did you decide?"

"I want the champagne macaron. Just one." She eyed my large bag pointedly.

"What? They're for Grandma."

"Liar."

"I mean, I'm going to have *some*. Two, tops. Plus one for Jake."

"Your grandmother is going to eat nine macarons?"

"She has a hollow leg, I swear."

"Whatever you say. Can we get back to bodies in the backyard? Promise me you will not go tromping around on private property looking for 'clues' like you're Velma."

"I don't think I'm Velma. She's too smart. I'm more of a Daphne, not looks-wise or anything, but just sort of walking around hoping the answer will reveal itself. I'm working on that though."

"Just don't be stupid, seriously."

"Who, me?"

Later that day I was thinking it might have been wise to listen to Alyssa as I drove up in front of a disheveled house on a dead-end street. It looked like the house of a man who had no craps to give.

It had been easy enough to find out about Margaret. There were a couple of news articles dated two years prior that she had gone missing after failing to pick her son up from daycare. She was an accountant and had left for a lunch meeting.

The ex was remarried already but I wasn't sure if he still lived here or not. It had the look of a rental house with inadequate lawn service. The bushes were massive, straining under the heavy snow.

"Bailey, Alyssa is right, this is stupid." Besides, it was cold, and what was I going to do, wander around the backyard with a shovel? That was about as probable a solution as ringing the doorbell and asking the guy if he killed his wife.

Neither was a solid plan. They weren't a plan at all, actually.

So I called Crimestoppers and gave an anonymous tip that Margaret's body was buried underneath the concrete patio and gave an address.

It occurred to me they could see what number I was calling

from but what choice did I have? I wasn't going to buy a burner phone just to give a tip.

"And how do you know this?" the responder asked, probably reading a script.

I hung up.

Knowing what I knew about crime solving, they weren't going to jump right all over this. It would be filed and given attention when there was time permitting.

Most likely it would be months before anyone on the department got around to seeing if my tip had any merit.

But by then it would be spring and the ground would no longer be frozen.

It was a start, though in the meantime I would do more digging for Margaret's sake. Ugh. I shouldn't think in terms of words like "digging."

Between Vera and Margaret, my view of backyard living was rapidly being tarnished.

There was a tap on my window and I almost jumped out of my skin.

"You okay?" a man in a thick coat and knit cap asked.

"Fine, yep, all good." I gave him a wave and put my car into drive and got the hell out of there.

TWELVE

"MOM, I don't know about this place... it seems a little too something for you." Young. It seemed too young for her. The entire building was designed for the needs of hipsters from the bike rack to the sustainable living (meaning no elevator) to the rooftop communal garden and cocktail lounge. I could not picture my mother discussing reducing her carbon footprint with a twenty-eight-year-old rock climber.

"I like it," she said, though her expression indicated she was lying.

"I think you're going to find you'll be happier in a building that is condo, not rental apartments." Everything was very bland. Very temporary. Then again, maybe that was what she wanted.

My mother didn't say anything. She just thanked the rental agent and gestured for me to follow her.

In the elevator, she said, "Next. I want more amenities."

"I agree. An indoor pool would be fantastic."

"So did you get a call from Tim?"

"Who's Tim?" I asked, drawing a blank.

She looked at me like I was nuts. "The prosecutor on the Nick Pitrello case. They should set a trial date this week, probably for July or August."

Ugh. Just what I wanted to think about. Not.

Let's recap. I found body parts in a field and a guy who was watching from his balcony came down to see why I was screaming. He asked me out. I went. He kidnapped me and confessed to killing three other people. But there was zero evidence to connect him to the murders, though they are still investigating and trying to build a case. He was being tried solely for kidnapping me so that would be a fun trial for me.

"Awesome. How long of a sentence do you think he'll get?"

"You're assuming he'll be found guilty."

"Well, he is guilty."

My mother gave me a withering look as we crossed the lobby. "Don't be naïve. If convicted I would guess five years, plus time served. Out in three."

Wonderful. "Thanks for the heads-up." I shivered as we stepped outside and it wasn't just from the cold. "Are you sure you're okay to do all this walking? That doesn't seem okay to me."

"I'm fine. I'm off work for another week still. They won't let me come back."

At least someone had sense. "Good. You need the rest."

"I'm bored out of my mind and I don't like any of these places we've looked at."

This was the sixth place and I was exhausted. Mom looked fine, but I was worn out from her disgust over carpet and oak cabinets. We still had four more places before we got to Devin Whittaker's condo. "Maybe you need to take a week off from searching and think about what you really want." I wasn't convinced she knew what she was looking for, exactly.

"No." She tugged her hat down over her ears and charged down the sidewalk. "I can't stand living in that house. Everywhere I look I see your father."

Which was quite a feat given Dad was in Florida and my mother would put Marie Kondo to shame with her decluttering. There had never been evidence of my father in the house for more than five minutes before my mom either tossed it or put it away. As a child, I'd been stunned to go to friends' houses and discover they were actually allowed to have toys in the living room. Mine were sequestered in my bedroom. As for Dad's whiskey glasses and toothpicks? They never stood a chance.

"Why don't you go to an Airbnb or a hotel for a few weeks instead of trying to rush this process? This is a big decision."

My mother waited for me to unlocked my car as we approached it. Once we were inside with the heat running, she crossed her arms over her chest. "That's not a bad idea. But we might as well see the rest scheduled today."

An idea popped into my head and I wasn't sure why it hadn't occurred to me sooner. "Why don't you move into Vera's condo? It belongs to Grandma, or will whenever Vera's estate is processed, but you know she won't care. She doesn't want it."

I pulled out of the spot, handing my phone to my mother so she could plug the next address into the GPS.

"I don't know. I never thought about going east."

"It's very close to your office. You won't have to buy it either. That might be a good thing at least for six months or so until everything is, you know, sorted out." Until her divorce from my father, is what I meant. Her thirty-year marriage that she was dissolving with the speed of light.

"I'd have to see it. How many bedrooms, how many bathrooms?"

"It's a three/two. I still have the key. I can take you over there after our last appointment."

"Why are you pushing this?" she asked, sniffing in suspicion.

Because I couldn't take months of house hunting with her. "I'm not. I'm just offering a solution. Or at least a temporary one. It's better than having to settle." You couldn't say "be impulsive" with my mother, she would hate being accused of that.

"It's not a bad idea," she said, begrudgingly. "So, are you really letting Grandma move in with you?"

"Yes. You know Dad. I don't think he can handle it." I really did. It was terrifying to think about him attempting to grocery shop to feed his mother. She would be living on cinnamon buns and whiskey if it were up to him.

"You've got that right." My mother sniffed.

I did feel bad for her. She was not exactly easy to live with, but it still had to be hard to realize your marriage was over. "And you need a break, Mom."

She made a noncommittal sound. "Then Jake is moving in with you? I don't know, Bailey. That's a lot of change all at once. That is a lot of people whose needs have to be met."

She had hit on my deepest fear and I didn't like that. "I like taking care of people," I said defensively. I was more nurturing than my mother. I wasn't like my sister of the four kids and fifth on the way, but I wasn't stone-cold like she could be. On the other hand, it was a lot of needs and I wasn't entirely sure if this arrangement would be meeting any of *mine*, but I kind of sort of didn't really have a choice. I mean, there's always a choice. I could look into assisted living for Grandma, but that wasn't the choice that was right for her, and how many more years before that was inevitable? I wanted her, and me, to enjoy time together while we could.

Living with Jake was scarier than living with Grandma. "Besides, it's not like I didn't talk to Jake about it first. Him moving in with me was actually his idea."

"What's the hurry?" she asked. "Get to know each other better. Make absolute certain you want to be with this man."

So this was about her, not me. "Hence the living together. This isn't marriage."

"Marriage isn't all it's cracked up to be."

"Why is it that you were thrilled that Jen was getting married but you're all negative about me moving in with Jake." That bugged me. "I've known Jake for eight years. It's not like he just appeared in my life the day we started dating."

"Don't be so sensitive," was her only response.

That was a total non-answer. Did she not like Jake? Or she just didn't trust me not to be an idiot? Ugh. Mothers. This was not what I should be stressing about when I felt convinced I was this close to solving Vera's murder. I felt it in my gut.

On TV they solved murders in forty-five minutes. Apparently, none of those detectives had mothers.

I pulled up in front of a condo building. "This is it. It looks like it's the end unit."

"No. Forget it. This is horrible," she said. "That house next door is completely run-down."

There was no point in arguing with her. "Okay," I said, pulling away. "Next."

We tore through the other places in record time and got back to Winton Place to view Devin Whittaker's condo.

"We were at this building three hours ago," she complained.

Trust me, I knew that. "Different unit."

"For crying out loud, why didn't we just see it then?"

"I don't know. The agent said seven."

"Christ," was her opinion on that.

Grateful my grandmother wasn't with us to be horrified at my mother's language, I just made a noncommittal sound.

The agent let us in and gave the usual speech. Then she started following us, which was counterproductive to my intention to snoop. But rest assured, my mother could handle that.

"Do you mind?" she asked. "I'd really just like to go through the condo on my own. You can wait right here by the door."

The agent looked floored. But really, who wants the agent trailing behind pointing out features? No one. Or at least not most someones. "Oh, I see. Of course." She sounded like she'd eaten a huge hunk of lemon. Sour.

The living room was staged, and I had to admit, I admired the stager's work. It was a good, clean design that respected the boxy shape of the condo. Everything was very modern. Sleek lines, pops of color with modern art. No personal photos or anything like that.

I opened the cabinets in the kitchen expecting to see what, I had no idea. I was starting to realize this, like much of my investigative attempts, was ill-fated. It wasn't like he was going to have something with Vera's name on it lying on the counter.

"This kitchen is nice," I said to my mother.

"It is," she said begrudgingly. "But I don't think I like being this high up."

"But at the other place you said it was too low."

The look she gave me could have sliced through steel. Instead of replying she went down the hall to the bedrooms.

I went into the bathroom and admired the finishes. Floating walnut vanity. Nice.

There was no medicine cabinet to peek into so I settled for sliding out a drawer. There were half a dozen pill bottles rolling around in there. As the label rolled into focus something caught my eye.

Vera Rosenbaum.

Hot damn.

Devin Whittaker had stolen pills from Vera. It didn't prove murder but it did prove that he had been in contact with her. Gingerly I picked one up using my fuzzy scarf and the cap and bottom so as not to interfere with fingerprints, or leave my own. The prescription had been filled in early December and it was for a well-known pain pill that happens to be highly addictive.

Interesting.

"Bailey?" my mother called. "Come look at this."

I shut the drawer and followed the sound of her voice, assuming she was going to criticize the view or the blinds or the lack of closet space.

Instead, she was pointing to the one and only personal photo in the whole condo. It was in a simple frame, resting on the chest of drawers.

"Who owns this place, Vera's love child?" she asked. "Look, she's in this picture."

Sure as shooting she was. I gasped. It was Tight Sweater Guy, aka Devin Whittaker, with Vera outside under the giant chandelier in the theater district.

And on the other side of Tight Sweater Guy was none other than Stanley Robertson.

Which made me almost certain one or both of them had killed Vera.

Suddenly nervous, I glanced around the bedroom like Stanley or Devin might pop up from under the bed. Which was possible because it was pretty damn clear Stanley wasn't at the Ritz or back in L.A.

"That's a crazy coincidence," I said, failing to mention that I already knew who this condo belonged to and that he was in Vera's will. "That's her former stepson," I said, pointing to Stanley. "He lives in L.A."

"That makes it even stranger."

It did. And Vera had been flat-out MIA lately. I could ask her who the heck Devin was to her if she would ever show her face.

Office hours. I mentally eye-rolled. That book was way off base.

"It does. So what do you think of this condo?"

Mom shrugged. "I'm not feeling it. Maybe we should look at Vera's place." Mom was clearly disgusted with her options and had decided maybe I wasn't a complete moron and the idea had merit. I felt almost flattered. "Maybe this photo of her is a sign."

Okay, that was weird. The only signs my mother normally made note of was the tell that criminals had. She did not believe in the universe guiding her to do anything so her comment caught me off guard.

"Okay. Let's go."

Thirty minutes later we were pulling into Vera's condo. I wasn't sure how soon she would be able to move in given the circumstances of the estate, but I wasn't about to bring that up.

"Private, attached two-car garage," I said as we pulled up.

"I hate when the façade is all garage," she said.

Lord help me. "You wouldn't be buying it though, remember? Just a pit stop."

That was going to be my mantra.

We stepped inside, going through the front door, into the hushed stillness of the condo. I didn't think my mother would have any issues with Vera having passed away in the backyard. She'd seen far too much in her twenty years as a prosecutor to be unnerved or sentimental. "It has good light."

I jumped all over that. "Absolutely. For being a townhome and mid-January? Imagine what it would be like in the summer."

"Don't fuss over me, Bailey," she said. "You're giving me a migraine. Can you just go sit down somewhere and let me look by myself?"

She'd done me like the real estate agent. Fine by me. "Sure. I'll be in the kitchen."

I tugged my boots off, not wanting to ruin the carpet with snow slush. When I padded into the kitchen in my socks, I noticed immediately the medications were gone from the table. Who had taken those? Pam? It had been implied she loved herself some prescription drugs. But Eva presumably had had access as well. Stanley didn't strike me as a pill thief, but then again, I wasn't sure what a pill thief looked like. There could be any reason someone would take a handful of anxiety pills, from hard-core addiction to someone just seeing an opportunity to have a recreational zen day.

Taking pills for any number of reasons probably had absolutely nothing to do with Vera's death. I was seeking clues where there weren't any.

The pain killers Devin had was not a bottle I had noted the day after Vera's death. So if he had taken them and killed her, why wouldn't he have taken them all? And why were they gone now?

I sat down and looked around, wishing I could puzzle together what had happened. I had this idea forming that Stanley had popped over to Vera's unannounced, then had caught her off guard in the kitchen. Would it really be that hard for a large man to shove a tiny ancient woman out an open door? She didn't even have to open the door herself. He could have opened it and grabbed her and tossed her out.

What would he gain though?

I stood up and paced back and forth, gritting my teeth as I thought hard. I needed to figure this out. I wished I could talk to Vera but she didn't know anything about her death, so I suppose it didn't really matter.

Something caught my eye. In the sink there was a tea cup. Not a mug, but an actual tea cup and saucer in a floral pattern. Had that been there before? I tried to visualize what the kitchen had looked like that first night I'd gone to Vera's but I couldn't remember. I felt like I would have noticed it though.

Weird. But not unexplainable. People had been in and out of the condo.

Damn it.

I went back to the back door and threw it open, propping it open with a chair, so I didn't get caught outside the way Vera had. I checked the knob and the button wasn't pushed in, but I wasn't taking any chances. We'd had a heatwave of almost forty degrees and some sun in the past few days so the snow was deflated a little. That nice wet bottom snow with a crusty top. A portion of the patio pavers was visible, which wasn't the case before.

The snow pattern was no longer discernible but I did have photos of it. I was about to pull my phone out and look at them again when something on the patio glinted in the sun. Vera's earring? I bent over and picked it up. It was a cuff link.

Engraved with the initials SAR.

I stood straight up, heart racing. Stanley Richardson. I had no idea what his middle name was, but this has to be his cuff link. I recalled sitting at the cocktail lounge with him and Alyssa and him complaining that he hadn't realized his cuff link was missing. That had been Monday night. Vera was killed Saturday.

Holy evil stepson.

I was right. I had known it.

Vera didn't have a dog so there was absolutely no reason for Stanley to have been out on her patio.

Unless he had killed her.

"Figured it out, didn't you?" a voice came from behind me, sounding amused.

I whirled around, clutching the cuff link in my palm

It was Stanley, wielding a very large and dangerous knife.

A *knife*? The composer was standing there like the chef at a carving station on a cruise.

All satisfaction at having solved who the killer was evaporated because I hadn't seen that one coming.

THIRTEEN

"WHAT ARE YOU DOING HERE?" I said, trying to sound cool, calm, and collected. I cursed my fair skin for giving away my fear. I could tell my cheeks were beet red.

"Nice try," he said. "I know you spoke to my father. We haven't always been close but I keep close tabs on him now."

"So you've spoken to him recently?" I said, which was obvious. I was starting to shiver, despite my coat still being on. I was in socks on wet stone and Stanley was in the doorway blocking my entrance. Not smart.

"I speak to him every day. It's a bit painful sometimes but I have to keep up the idea that we've mended fences and everything is great. That he wasn't a negligent asshole of a father."

Stanley was dressed in lounge pants and a knit sweater. Even though I was transfixed by the giant knife in his hand, I realized he was also in socks, not shoes. Where the hell had he come from?

Then it all clicked. "You've been staying here, haven't you? I called the Ritz and they said you were never registered there."

His eyebrows shot up. "You called the Ritz? Clever girl. I didn't expect that from you."

"I'm starting to learn the criminal mind," I told him, hoping he would think I was as badass as I was clever.

"Then you know that I'm out of money. That should be pretty obvious."

Should be. I had to admit to myself I was about a beat behind since I should have realized the second he wasn't at the Ritz what the truth was. Then again, his father was eighty-eight. It was fair to conclude he was confused. "Very obvious," I said, going for brazen. "Though I have to admit it wasn't at first meet. It was only after I spoke to your father that the pieces fell into place."

I wish I had the ability to record what Stanley was saying but there was no way I could pull my phone out without him knowing what I was doing. I was also afraid to make any sudden moves. I did stick my hand in my pocket, fishing around for my phone.

His eyes followed my movement. "Going for your phone? Forget it, Red. Hands where I can see them."

It occurred to me he didn't realize my mother was with me. He must not have heard us come in together. I wasn't sure if that was good or bad. Sure, backup was handy but not if my mother had no clue we were in danger and hello, she'd just had a heart attack. A shock like seeing her daughter murdered would most likely kill her.

Pulling my hand back out, I said, "Calm down. I'm just cold."

"You made my father suspicious, you know. This would have all been as easy as taking candy from a baby. Make sure Vera is dead first, so I get the entirety of my father's estate when he dies. Can you believe my father is still carrying a torch for Vera after all these years? He left a million bucks to her in his will! That's my money. If she was dead when he dies, I get everything."

That's when I knew he was for sure planning to kill me because hello, he had just confessed everything to me. Though maybe he didn't think it would matter. That it was the perfect crime. Jake and Ryan had been right—it had always been all about the money.

"Your father seemed quite fond of Vera."

"She took him for a ride in the sixties and she was still taking him for a ride. I need that money. My father doesn't have that much left. Giving that kind of cash to an old lady, who is just going to croak, meaning her dumbass niece and nephew will get the money, makes no sense whatsoever."

That was fair in that I could see it might be frustrating to know fringe relatives by marriage would get your father's money, but that didn't mean you go and kill an old lady. Geez Louise. I eyeballed the knife, which had slackened in his grip.

"Plus, with everything rightly restored to me with Vera dying, I would also get whatever Vera would leave me. I had no idea if I was even in her will, though I thought it was possible. Let's be clear. It's not like I wanted to kill Vera– that was never the point, but once I realized she left me five grand I wasn't mad at myself for doing her in. I mean, that was just rude. Either cut me out or give me something that matters. Five thousand bucks was just a slap in the face. That won't even pay my liquor bill."

What the hell was he drinking? I don't think I'd spent a thousand dollars on alcohol in the entirety of my life, let alone five thousand. Then again, I'm generally okay with box wine, don't tell my mother.

"I'm sure she didn't mean it as an insult."

His face turned red and his hand shook as he waved the knife around, gripping it tightly again. My shoulders tensed.

"She had no family except for Dumb and Dumber, Eva and Steven. Way to make it clear I wasn't family after all. I wasn't singled out in any way. It was absolutely an insult."

"I'm sorry." I could see that might be hurtful but for the record, he hadn't known that when he shoved her into a snow pile. Clearly Vera had sensed his love wasn't exactly unconditional. "For what it's worth, I like you, Stanley."

"I like you, Stanley," he mocked, moving his head back and forth and speaking in a high-pitched voice.

For a guy who had hinted at being bullied he was making it very difficult to feel any sort of compassion.

"But even worse was that she left Devin the same measly five grand. I honestly never knew what a complete bitch she could be." He tilted his head. "Well. That's not entirely true. I knew she was a selfish, vain bitch, but I never cared because she liked me. But apparently not as much as I thought she did."

My teeth were chattering now, but at least it was in the thirties today. I could tough out a few more minutes. "Who is Devin to you?"

"Devin is Vera's son that she gave up for adoption. He's also my on-again, off-again lover."

"Vera has a son?" I asked, astonished. My mother's flippant comment was right.

"Yes, she got knocked up in the early seventies, or maybe late sixties, I'm foggy on the details. Some Cuban guy when she was partying in Miami Beach with Frank Sinatra's crowd. He was her valet guy."

That was full-service parking, geez. "But... how does Devin know Vera?"

"Since she was an advanced age for giving birth, the adoptive parents insisting on knowing her name. Devin looked her up around ten years ago and she was mildly intrigued by him. She introduced us and we would see each other whenever I was in town."

"Why aren't you staying with Devin?"

"Oh, honey, please. I need my space."

"Was Devin following me? Did he punch me?"

Stanley clucked a little. "Yes. Sorry about that. I asked him to keep an eye on you since you were asking so many questions. But he panicked that you recognized him and swung. Not a quick thinker."

I shifted a little on the balls of my feet. I was getting concerned my socks would freeze to the patio. "So what's the plan here, Stanley? Why do you have a knife in your hand?" That was something I had learned, but rarely implemented, from my mother. Cut to the chase. Put someone on the spot so you regain some control.

"I could let you go and assume you'll keep your mouth shut."

"Yes, let's do that."

"But what I think makes more sense is for me to kill you."

Bad plan. "Here, at Vera's? That doesn't seem wise. Knives are very bloody. Besides, your DNA has to be all over this place since you've been squatting here."

"I'm not going to stab you. Do I look like the Black Dahlia? That sounds messy and frankly disturbing, given that I'm new to murder."

I was starting to fear that my mother had been killed by Stanley before he had appeared at the patio door. Where the hell was she? I would never forgive myself if my insistence on her seeing Vera's condo wound up killing her.

"No knife is reassuring to me. Am I going to freeze to death too?"

"Vera was drugged by me first, then shoved outside at night with no cell phone. I don't think that applies here since you're able-bodied and have your wits about you."

"In theory."

He laughed. "This is a shame. I really do enjoy your company. Hand me your phone."

Begrudgingly, I pulled it out of my pocket. I was going to have to rush him. There was no other option. Or run. Given the knife situation I opted for run. I threw my phone, hitting him in the face, and took off to the neighbor's back door. I pounded on it frantically, but realized even if the neighbor heard me, Stanley was mere feet away. I kept running until I reached the very end of the row of townhomes, and darted around the side of the units. I would have thought he would catch me given I was in socks, but then I realized he wasn't even chasing me anymore.

Crap. He was going to cut through the house.

But I had my car keys in my pocket. I didn't have my mother, but I had my keys and if he was coming out the front door, at least he was away from her. I spotted him in the doorway looking left and right. When he was searching in the opposite direction, I scooted to the back of my car and in a painful squat position shifted myself along the driver's side of the car. I opened the door and jumped in, clicking the lock button. I could hear him yelling profanities at me.

I turned the engine on as he ran down the walkway and tried to open my door. He banged on the glass.

"Get away from me!" I yelled. I didn't have my phone so I couldn't call the cops. I couldn't leave without my mother. This was awkward. He looked very menacing with that knife in his hand.

"It looks like you have everything under control," Ryan said, appearing in the passenger seat. "Not."

"I don't need you running commentary."

"Drop the knife and step away from my daughter," my mother said, standing in the walkway pointing a gun at Stanley.

He dropped the knife, startled. "Holy hell. Don't point that thing at me!"

"Get in the house," she said, moving slowly, her grip steady.

"Your mother is cooler than you," Ryan said.

She kind of was. But I have a good personality. "Shut up."

Stanley wasn't as smart as he appeared to be. He took off running down the driveway. My mother fired the gun into the air. He screamed and dropped to the ground, blubbering and crying.

"Oh for chrissake," she said, gun in one hand and phone in the other. "Drama queen."

I shoved open the car door and jumped on Stanley's back. He let out another scream and tried to buck me off but I used my thighs to clamp on. It was like bull riding. If bulls wore cashmere sweaters and squealed like a pig. I tied his wrists together with my scarf, just to ensure he couldn't easily escape. Then I grabbed the knife and threw it in the backseat of my car. The child locks were on so Stanley would have to go through the front and climb into the back to retrieve it and I didn't see that happening.

Just to be on the safe side though, I called my mother over frantically. "Get in until the cops get here."

She looked thoroughly unperturbed for a woman who'd recently had a heart attack.

Mom got in and frowned when she sat on Ryan, like she felt something.

"Dude, your mom is sitting in my lap. This is so freaky."

"Are you okay?" she asked. "I heard half of what that idiot was saying. Who kills an old woman like that? The bastard. God, it's a shame I won't be assigned this case when it comes to trial. I want to nail him to the wall."

"Do you always carry a gun?" I asked, though I wasn't sure I wanted the answer.

"Real estate is sketchy, Bailey. I like to be prepared."

I peeked out to make sure Stanley was still there. He was gone, Michael Myers style.

I turned around and didn't see anything. When I turned back, he was staring at me. "Ack!" I shouted, before I could stop myself. Then I rolled down the window and slapped him. Vera style. Like was written about in the letters. "How dare you," I said, and I felt bold. Confident.

"Atta girl," Vera told me from the back seat.

I rolled the window back up and turned to her. I gave her a wink. "That was for Vera."

"Your monthly quota stands at one," Ryan said, pretending to wrap his arms around my mother from behind, which was profoundly disturbing.

"Don't do that," I snapped before I could stop myself.

He just shrugged. "It's a ghost's life, what can I say?"

"Bailey, roll the window back up. I don't want to have to shoot him. He seems to have undone his scarf restraints."

He had. Stanley was running back into the house, probably for his phone to call a car service, when the cops pulled in. My mother got out to speak to them and I let her.

I turned the heat on in my car to warm my feet up. "I should have hit him with my car," I told Ryan.

"Nah. You don't want that on your conscience."

FOURTEEN

"ARE WE DOING THIS?" I asked Jake, raising my glass of wine to my lips.

"Yeah, why not? We could use a vacation, especially since you had Stanley pull a knife on you."

"That was a rough day," I admitted. "Mom was so difficult, and then there was Stanley, confessing to murder."

Grandma was having dinner with my father, who was back from his golf trip with Judy. Jake and I had just eaten sea bass, inspired by Alyssa, who had posted eight photos of her dinner triumph on Instagram.

"I can't believe that guy," Jake said, shaking his head. "After he told you that Vera was so supportive of him as a teenager."

"Right? Talk about the worst payback ever. At least Devin confessed immediately to assaulting me."

"Total wimp. He rolled under ten minutes of interrogation."

"At least he didn't kill anyone."

"He hit you though. Not exactly a Boy Scout. He's lucky they didn't leave me alone in the room with him." Jake's nostrils flared just talking about me getting hit.

I sipped my wine and decided to change the subject back to

sunshine and sex with no elderly women in the house. "Hit the button. Buy the plane tickets."

"Why don't you do it?"

"I'm scared. I haven't taken a vacation in forever."

"Me either." His finger hovered over the button. "You're sure?"

I pictured salsa dancing with Jake (though neither one of us salsa danced), fruity cocktails, the Hemingway house, and key lime pie. "I'm positive."

He hit the button and the processing notice came up. Then the notice that we were booked on a flight.

"That's it. We have a flight and they have our money. We're going to Key West in four weeks." Jake grinned at me and sipped his whiskey. "That feels like freedom right there, baby."

"It does, doesn't it? No more winter. No more parents. No more ghosts." The idea was exhilarating. "I need a bathing suit."

"Bikini, please. If I can make a request."

"We'll see." I was more a one-piece kind of girl. I was picturing something retro inspired, me frolicking in the pool, riding a swan float.

"I just had a thought," Jake said. "Isn't Key West one of the most haunted cities in the US?"

My fantasy came screeching to a halt. "What? Are you serious?"

He nodded. "I think so."

I grabbed the computer and did a search on top haunted cities in the country. New Orleans. Savannah. St. Augustine. Key West.

"Holy crap, that is not good."

Jake gave that familiar shrug. "It won't be a big deal. It will be fun."

Sure. As fun as when the boys shot spitballs onto me the whole bus ride home in the fifth grade.

I chugged the rest of my wine. "Better ghosts with sunshine than ghosts with snow."

"Bright side, babe. That's what I love about you."

More like neurotic, but he could believe whatever he wanted

about me, as long as it was positive. "I guess I better finish my book about learning to be a medium."

"Maybe we should make flash cards and I'll quiz you."

That made me grin. "Not a bad idea."

"I told you, all my ideas are good ones."

I slapped the laptop lid shut and slid closer to him. "They truly are."

The front door opened. "We're back," my father shouted in a booming voice.

Jake sighed.

Ryan appeared behind him. Grandma shuffled into the kitchen. "We're not interrupting, are we?"

"Not at all," Jake said.

"Four weeks," I whispered to him.

Ghosts or not, we were going to Key West and there was a lounge chair with my name on it.

Especially since Margaret was now standing next to Ryan, waving enthusiastically at me.

A day in the life of the world's crappiest medium.

That's me.

Thank you for reading It's a Ghost's Life! Coming soon... Bailey's adventures in Key West with her skeptical boyfriend Marner in
GHOSTS LIKE IT HOT.

ABOUT THE AUTHOR

USA Today and New York Times Bestselling author Erin McCarthy sold her first book in 2002 and has since written over seventy novels and novellas in teen fiction, romance, and mysteries. Erin has a special weakness for tattoos, high-heeled boots, bagpipes, Frank Sinatra, and martinis. She lives with her husband and their blended family of kids and rescue dogs.

Connect with Erin:
www.erinmccarthymysteries.com

ALSO BY ERIN MCCARTHY

GONE WITH THE GHOST
SILENCE OF THE GHOST
ONCE UPON A GHOST
HOW THE GHOST STOLE CHRISTMAS (Holiday novella)
IT'S A GHOST'S LIFE
GHOSTS LIKE IT HOT
DANCES WITH GHOSTS

Made in the USA
Monee, IL
02 August 2022